REA

"YOU

ACPL ITEM

DISCARDED

"Why ever n...

Sighing, Miles turned back toward the darkness. "I have my work here."

Disappointment washed over Mellie, but she couldn't very well argue with the same excuse she'd given her family when they'd suggested she leave the Park. "Well, now you know how I feel—except *you* get to do exactly as you please."

"You think so?" He peered at her out of the corner of his eye.

"You get to stay here and dig, don't you—while I'm forced to go to town?"

"Perhaps I truly want to go to the exhibition, but I think my work here is too important to abandon."

He's quizzing me again, Mellie thought. She grinned at him. "Are you trying to tell me that *his lordship, the only child,* doesn't always do exactly as he pleases?"

His gaze flitted over her face. "Never, lately, it seems."

The intensity in his eyes made her draw in her breath. "What have you been wanting to do?"

He studied her for a moment longer, and despite her inexperience she knew he wanted what she did.

"Only this." Stepping toward her, he bent and met her mouth with his. . . .

BOOK YOUR PLACE ON OUR WEBSITE AND MAKE THE READING CONNECTION!

We've created a customized website just for our very special readers, where you can get the inside scoop on everything that's going on with Zebra, Pinnacle and Kensington books.

When you come online, you'll have the exciting opportunity to:

- View covers of upcoming books
- Read sample chapters
- Learn about our future publishing schedule (listed by publication month *and author*)
- Find out when your favorite authors will be visiting a city near you
- Search for and order backlist books from our online catalog
- Check out author bios and background information
- Send e-mail to your favorite authors
- Meet the Kensington staff online
- Join us in weekly chats with authors, readers and other guests
- Get writing guidelines
- AND MUCH MORE!

**Visit our website at
http://www.kensingtonbooks.com**

LORD
ST. LEGER'S
FIND

Jennifer Malin

ZEBRA BOOKS
KENSINGTON PUBLISHING CORP.

http://www.kensingtonbooks.com

ZEBRA BOOKS are published by

Kensington Publishing Corp.
850 Third Avenue
New York, NY 10022

Copyright © 2002 by Jennifer Zorger

All rights reserved. No part of this book may be reproduced in any form or by any means without the prior written consent of the Publisher, excepting brief quotes used in reviews.

If you purchased this book without a cover you should be aware that this book is stolen property. It was reported as "unsold and destroyed" to the Publisher and neither the Author nor the Publisher has received any payment for this "stripped book."

All Kensington titles, imprints and distributed lines are available at special quantity discounts for bulk purchases for sales promotion, premiums, fund-raising, educational or institutional use.

Special book excerpts or customized printings can also be created to fit specific needs. For details, write or phone the office of the Kensington Special Sales Manager: Kensington Publishing Corp., 850 Third Avenue, New York, NY 10022. Attn. Special Sales Department. Phone: 1-800-221-2647.

Zebra and the Z logo Reg. U.S. Pat. & TM Off.

First Printing: December 2002
10 9 8 7 6 5 4 3 2 1

Printed in the United States of America

One

Miles Kennestone, Lord St. Leger, guided his pair of grays through the gates of Lowery Park. From the road the estate looked much as he remembered it from his only other visit, five years ago. The white gravel drive glowed in the afternoon sun, dappled with shade at regular intervals by the scattered oaks lining both sides.

"There is nothing like spring in Dorset," his friend Ben Romney said, sitting beside him on the box of the carriage. "I love arriving here at this time of the year."

Through the foliage Miles spotted the gatehouse where he and Ben had lodged in the past and were slated to stay again this time. The layout of the interior flooded back to him as clearly as if he had left only weeks ago. He hadn't thought about the cozy cottage in years, but now he recalled that he had truly enjoyed its peace and quiet.

Too bad he had found so little serenity elsewhere on the estate. The memory of the Lowery girls' antics stirred up a sick feeling in his stomach.

"I don't suppose we could go directly to the gate-house," he said, knowing full well they could not.

"I say, Miles, 'twouldn't be good form to defer our host's greeting." Ben looked at him, pushing a pair of wire-framed spectacles up on his thin nose. "Besides, why would you want to? Don't you want to hear what progress Sir William has made on the villa since his last letter?"

"Of course I do." He avoided his friend's gaze, staring ahead at the drive. "But I have unpleasant memories associated with the main house. In fact, I can scarcely believe I let you persuade me to come back here."

"Nonsense. You said you would rather spend the spring in archaeological pursuit than being pursued by debutantes in London. Well, there is no better Romano-British site in the country than the Lowery villa."

"True, but the last time I was here, I didn't succeed in escaping the husband hunters."

Ben pursed his lips. "As I've already assured you, there will be no repeat of the folly you encountered then. I have returned every summer since, and my stays have been entirely filled with scholarly matters."

"I hope you're painting an accurate picture," Miles said, slowing the horses but continuing up the drive. "Your studious nature sometimes makes you oblivious to life's less academic matters, such as the wiles of women. I wish I could be as focused as you, but I am not. If I detect the first hint of trouble to come, I will be packed and gone before you can say 'Great Caesar's ghost.' "

"Your loss. Personally, I have been dying to get back to work on the mosaic Sir William and I came across last autumn." Ben sat up straighter on the box, stretching his neck to survey the parkland. "I wish I could see the dig from here. Sir William says his servants have already removed the tarp they placed over the area for the winter. Now they're constructing a tent over a portion to provide shade for our work.''

Miles lifted his eyebrows, his misgivings somewhat softened by such attention to detail. ''I have to admit that Sir William is an accommodating host. 'Tis a great advantage when the landowner at a site takes an interest in archaeology himself. And there's no denying that the man is master of some of the best-preserved ruins in England. 'Tis only his husband-hunting daughters that give me pause.''

Ben let out a sigh. ''I have told you they are gone—married and living far off in the West Indies.''

He acknowledged that his friend had repeated his assurances several times. ''Indeed, you have.''

The carriage rounded a curve, and the main house came within view. Long rays of sunshine lit up the marble columns on the facade. In the beautiful spring weather, the neoclassical manor looked as glorious as Miles imagined the Parthenon must have in its prime.

His uneasiness resurged as they approached the portico. This was the spot where Euterpe, Sir William Lowery's middle daughter, had often accosted him in the past. Invariably clad in a low-cut gown, she would make a show of bending down to look at whatever artifact he carried. Other times she would insist on fussing over some article of his work-stained clothing. The woman was the most voracious coquette he had ever encountered outside of London.

As he pulled up to the house, he couldn't help but note, ''I only hope the Lowery girls don't show up for a visit while we're here.''

''Clio and Euterpe have not set foot in the Park for years—though, naturally, I cannot guarantee they won't sail to England this summer.'' Ben leaned forward, ready to jump out of his seat before the barouche had even stopped. Looking up toward the front door, he grinned. "Of course, Mellie will be here, as always. I look forward to seeing her."

The statement stunned Miles. He halted the grays more abruptly than he meant to. "What do you mean 'Mellie will be here'?"

Ben's body lurched forward. He grabbed the backrest to steady himself. Turning to Miles, he curled his lip. "Nice bit of driving there, chap."

"Never mind that. What did you say about Melpomene?"

He adjusted his spectacles again. "Mellie still lives at home. 'Tis the other two who are gone."

Heat rose under Miles' collar. He glared at his friend. "Then why have you been telling me, up until two minutes ago, that Sir William's progeny were all married off? If I knew any of his daughters were here, I never would have agreed to come."

Ben blinked back at him, silent, as if astounded.

"Don't you have anything to say for yourself?" he asked. "If you were lying to me to secure my help with that mosaic, I promise you I won't stand for it."

"I wasn't lying." He glowered and jumped off the box, snatching the reins from Miles' lifeless hands. "How was I to know you were lumping Mellie in with her sisters? *She* is hardly a husband hunter. Clio and Euterpe were the ones obsessed with that sort of thing. I will thank you to withdraw your accusation."

Miles dropped his gaze. The misunderstanding irked him to no end, but he regretted his hasty choice of words. Ben was many things, and none of them a liar. "Forgive me. Admittedly, the elder sisters were the coquettes, particularly Euterpe."

"Well, they are gone, exactly as I said." He twisted the reins around a post and tied them. "Rest assured you will be quite safe from their advances."

"I only wish I'd asked you for more details before,"

he muttered. Climbing down to the ground, he glanced nervously at the manor. "Perhaps Melpomene is not a husband hunter. I don't know. She was too young for that last time I was here. But the fact remains that she's an intrusive, bumbling little hoyden with the run of her father's estate. Surely you remember what she did to my Minerva-Sulis pot? The chit should be kept under lock and key."

"You won't think so when you meet her again." Ben gave his knot a final yank and dusted off his hands. "That was five years ago. Perhaps she was a bit excitable, but anyone could have dropped that pot. Frankly, at the time, I thought you were damn hard on her."

"An archaeological dig is no place for a child."

"Well, she's a grown woman now—and a skilled archaeologist, too. Quite up on her education. I sometimes even go to her with questions about artifacts. You will be surprised by her—and impressed, I think."

Before Miles could repeat his doubts, Sir William emerged from the house, followed by two footmen. A distinguished-looking man of about sixty, the baronet radiated good health, which he demonstrated by dashing down the front steps.

"Good to see you, Bennie. The mosaic awaits you. Miles, always a pleasure." He turned to the servants. "Smith, Stone, take their belongings to the gatehouse, then drive the gig around to the stables."

Miles stepped forward while his friend shook their host's hand. He was glad to note that no females flitted out onto the portico after Sir William. Ben seemed to be correct about the husband hunters being gone. If Euterpe had been present, there would have been no holding her back.

Sir William turned to him and extended his hand. "I'm delighted you could join us this year, Miles. We have missed your expertise. Come into the house and tell me what pursuits have kept you away for so long."

"Well, I spent most of last summer at a Saxon site in Devon, and I have visited a few other prehistoric digs up north." As they climbed the front steps, he named a number of places that sounded singularly unimpressive to his own ears. Any Romano-British archaeologist worth his salt knew that Lowery Park was among the richest sites in the country.

As the three of them entered the hall, Sir William continued to ask him polite questions. The interior of the house was a decorative marvel, adorned with a wealth of classical statuary—some authentic pieces, others fine reproductions. The baronet and Miles' late father had fought together against Bonaparte's army in Egypt, where both had gained an interest in antiquities, which Miles had inherited.

They settled into Sir William's library, a well-stocked room that smelled pleasantly of seasoned leather. The baronet poured a round of brandy.

Miles waited till each man had a snifter, then lifted his with a tentative smile. "To our host."

As they drank, a warm feeling welled up inside him, one that had nothing to do with the alcohol. He had to admit that Lowery Park had a delightful atmosphere . . . when the women of the family were absent.

"Thank you for inviting us," he said. "Your hospitality is much appreciated."

"My pleasure."

Ben tossed off a second swig, then asked the baronet, "How are your daughters doing?"

"All well, thank you." Sir William leaned back in his armchair. "You'll see that Mellie is as lively as ever. She is out in the field, of course. I exhorted her to come in and dress to greet you properly, but she won't be dragged away from her endeavors."

3 1833 04009 068 7

"Is she working on the mosaic?" Ben asked.

"Oh, no. She has another area she has been excavating. She is always determined to be independent." The baronet frowned into his drink.

Ben didn't seem to catch the hint of reservation. "You must be very proud of her accomplishments."

"I am . . ." The older man's voice trailed off.

Miles could almost hear the "but" in his thoughts. "Pardon me, Sir William, but if something is troubling you and Ben and I might be able to help, please don't hesitate to ask."

The baronet sighed. "I am embarrassed to bring up my deficiencies. Then again, during your visit here, you may well come to the same conclusion I have— a possibility just as mortifying. You see, I am beginning to fear I have done Mellie a disservice by allowing her her whims all of these years."

"Nonsense." Ben's eyes were wide, as if the suggestion shocked him. "Your daughter has become a skilled archaeologist. Who would have thought any woman would be so determined to distinguish herself in a scholarly field?"

"But that is the problem." Sir William set down his snifter, lines furrowing his brow. "Is archeology an appropriate pursuit for a woman? When she was a child and followed me into the fields, the neighbors looked on with amusement. But these days I notice that their looks have become rather hostile. Other young ladies in the village barely speak to her. She leads an almost solitary existence."

Miles rubbed his chin. "Is there an older woman you could confide in who could perhaps act as a mentor to her?"

"Our housekeeper, Mrs. Burke, has tried, but she simply doesn't have the influence with Mellie. I used to believe that a visit from one of her sisters would do the trick, but lately I fear even that won't help." Sir William sighed and picked up his glass. " 'Tis a shame that Clio and Euterpe have been absent these four years. Those two are the picture of femininity, just like their mother. If only my dear Catherine had lived longer, Mellie might have turned out more like them."

Miles shot an appalled glance at Ben and turned back to his host. "You are much too hard on yourself, sir."

"Mellie is a fine woman," Ben broke in, perhaps afraid his friend would say something untoward about the other daughters. "I can't think of another female I would rather hold a conversation with."

"That is kind of you to say, Ben, and I know you are sincere—but I wonder how many men in our society would share your views."

A bang from out in the hall made Miles jump—a door slamming, he judged, once he had regained his bearings. Hurried footsteps followed, and a throaty feminine voice sang out, "Where is he? Where is he? Bennie?"

Ben stood up and looked past Miles to the hall door. His eyes lit up. "Mellie, how good to see you!"

Miles began to rise, too, glancing over his shoulder toward her. The sight greeting him knocked him back into his seat. A slim beauty stood in the doorway, long red hair tumbling down over her shoulders. She was shockingly clad in a loose-fitting smock and a pair of boy's riding breeches. As she stepped forward to take both of Ben's hands in hers, the leather pants revealed every provocative contour of her hips and thighs.

Never in his life had he seen such an outrageous display of feminine charms. Two thoughts screamed in his mind: She was scandalous . . . and she was exquisite. He was well and truly shocked—and, despite himself, aroused.

Recalling his manners, he scrambled to his feet. As she looked to him, he bowed, more deeply than he would have under normal circumstances. Perhaps he was trying to make up for her lack of form by padding his own.

When she recognized him, the smile fled her face. Her turquoise eyes seemed to lose their luster. "Lord St. Leger, I didn't realize you were coming, too."

His tongue nearly failed him. His wits did entirely. "How do you do, Miss Lowery?"

"Fine, thank you." There was an awkward pause, then she curtsied—a ridiculous gesture, dressed as she was. "Welcome to Lowery Park. Will you be staying all summer?"

Her distant manner gave him the impression she was as wary of his coming as he was. He told himself it was unlikely. She had been little more than a child when he had last seen her. Five years was a long time in a young person's life, as her appearance illustrated. Actually, he was surprised she even remembered him. "Yes, in the gatehouse, with Ben."

"Can you sit with us, Mellie?" Sir William asked. "I was about to update Ben on the mosaic."

She glanced at Miles, then looked back to her father. "I am afraid I cannot at the moment. I need to get back out to the field."

"Surely you can call it a day, under the circumstances."

She shook her head. "You know I need to get as much done as I can before Wednesday. I only came up to the house because I ran out of bracing timbers."

Despite the change in her appearance, she seemed to be the same spoiled little girl Miles had known years ago. He watched with the other men as she hurried across the room to a stack of firewood, pulling out the longest log.

"You don't mean to use that?" her father asked.

"I've sent James into the village for proper lumber, but this will have to do for now." She grabbed a second log from the pile and started back toward the door.

Miles frowned. Her carelessness remained unchanged, too—but then that should have been obvious with one look at her. A woman so heedless about exposing her charms wasn't likely to be fastidious in other regards.

"You won't be long, will you?" Sir William asked. "Dinner is set for eight."

"I shall be back in time."

The baronet looked to Miles and Ben. "Is eight good for you, too? I insist you eat with us tonight."

"We'd love to," Ben said. He smiled at Mellie. "That will give you a chance to tell us all about your project."

The smile she returned didn't quite reach her eyes. Once more, she stole a glance at Miles before looking back to Ben. "It will be a pleasure. Till then."

She curtsied again and turned. As she walked out of the room, Miles couldn't help but watch every move she made—how her hips swayed, how the leather of her breeches stretched over the curve of her bottom and outlined the feminine form of her legs. Her high black riding boots looked stylish in a strange, utterly foreign way. In another time or in some distant culture she might have been a celebrated beauty. He had never encountered anything like her. Despite himself, he was fascinated.

"So where do we stand on the mosaic?" Ben asked Sir William. "Pardon the pun. I mean, how much of the piece is exposed?"

"Little more than you saw last autumn. We had such a cold winter that the ground was quite hard. Mellie and I didn't dare do much excavating, for fear of cracking buried artifacts."

As the two other men spoke, Miles glimpsed Mellie passing by the window. She now carried a large leather satchel on one shoulder and walked with long, graceful strides. As she moved out of sight, he again thought she seemed to belong among some other people—the ancient Saxons, perhaps, or the Bretons.

"You look a bit dazed, Miles," Sir William said.

"Hmm?" He spun around. "Oh, yes. Forgive me. I suppose I'm tired after the journey here."

"Of course. You lads should take some time to settle into the gatehouse now. We can continue our discussion at dinner."

Ben looked down at his clothing. "It *would* be good to get out of this dusty gear."

"Indeed, I could stand to collect myself, too," Miles said. The understatement of his words struck him. What was he thinking, ogling one of the Lowery girls—one who dressed and behaved with no regard for convention? He had to get his mind back on his work.

Sir William showed them to the front door, shaking hands with them again.

The two men set off toward a wooded area to one side of the drive. As they turned down a gravel path that led to the gatehouse, Miles tried to think of a question about the villa to ask his friend, but he couldn't seem to get past the outrageous image of Melpomene that had been burned into his mind.

"Mellie didn't seem herself," Ben said. "You likely wouldn't perceive it, having not seen her for so long, but there was something strange about her."

"Could it have been her clothing?" His annoyance with the situation—and with himself—crept into his tone. "The woman was dressed like a hoyden."

"More like a stableboy, I'd say. I've seen her dressed that way before on occasions when she is deeply involved in a project. Surely you don't expect her to wear a ball gown while sifting through dirt in the field?"

"Not a ball gown, naturally, but perhaps a riding habit or a traveling costume. She is a *woman*, for heaven's sake, not a boy. Did you see the way those breeches clung to her? To every curve on her body?"

"I can't say I noticed. I mean, who thinks of Mellie that way?" Suddenly Ben turned his head and studied him more closely. *"You* do?"

"Don't be absurd." He grimaced and looked ahead at the gravel trail. "As you well know, I am here to think about archaeological matters, not to waste my efforts on women and their wiles."

"Mellie has no wiles."

"Forgive me if I suggest you may be naive, Ben. Given who her sisters are, I daresay she is chockful of wiles. She may even dress the way she does purposely to entice men."

His friend let out a snort. "Once you've seen her at work, you'll realize that her costume is utterly practical."

"I have no desire to observe her further." He kicked a large stone out of his path. "If I wanted to discuss women and their clothing, I would have gone into London for the Season, not come here."

"You're the one who brought it up."

He scowled. "Well, I shan't again. First thing tomorrow morning, I intend to get out to the field and set my mind to more useful matters."

From the corner of his eye, he saw Ben shake his head. "About time, if you ask me."

Evidently his friend still believed he was attaching too much weight to Melpomene's presence at the Park. Was he truly overreacting?

Hoping Ben was right, he made a private vow not to open the topic again—at least not again that evening.

Two

"Oh, no!"

Melpomene Lowery snatched her arm from a small tunnel just as its dirt ceiling collapsed. The sight of the sudden mess before her made her wince. On any other day the cave-in would be only a minor impediment, but today she could ill afford the extra work it meant.

"Blast it!" Coughing on stirred-up dust, she rose from her stooped position and resisted the urge to stamp her foot. One did not stamp at an archaeological site, and as she had observed in the field since her childhood, she was well aware of the protocol.

She gave the damage a quick appraisal and sighed in resignation. At least the setback afforded her a moment to stretch her poor, stiff limbs. She loved the challenge of digging up history, but the constant bending could be back-breaking, and the late-March morning boasted an unseasonable warmth that added nothing to her comfort.

"Miss Mellie?"

The interruption from above the trench where she

stood came as no surprise. Though the ruins of the Roman villa sat within the bounds of her father's estate, Sir William insisted that a servant attend her whenever she dug. Still frowning toward the area of the mishap, she responded absently, "Yes, James?"

"You all right down there?" the young groom asked, leaning over a mound of dirt that topped her head. "I thought I heard you holler."

She waved off his concern, lifting her face to squint up at his sun-haloed features. "I'm fine. I shouted because the shaft I've been excavating all morning collapsed. Naturally, it happened just as I had my hand on the final portion of this pot." She gestured toward a large ceramic vessel lying in several pieces on the ground. "Can anything else go wrong today? I seem to be getting nowhere."

He pursed his lips. "I'm awful sorry, miss. Was something wrong with the boards I fetched for you yesterday?"

She shook her head and tucked an escaping strand of hair back under her chip-straw hat, an accessory sharply mismatched to the boy's breeches and man's shirt she wore. "No, it's my own fault. I'm afraid I didn't brace the tunnel well enough."

"Should I dig the hole back out for you?"

"Thank you, but I prefer to do it myself." She stooped back down and reached for a trowel and a sieve. "Normally, I would have done a proper job of the bracing, but I've been rushing about to get as much done as possible before my sister arrives tomorrow."

"Lady Moorehead never did take kindly to your diggin', did she?"

"Hardly. And I daresay that even living in the West Indies for these past four years hasn't changed her views." Mellie realized she had said more than she should, but the groom had practically grown up in

Lowery Park and would already have an idea of what kind of strife her sister had caused her before marrying. Archaeology was only one of many activities Terry found unfitting for Mellie.

"She means well, of course," she added with a tight smile. "Since our mother did not live to shape me into a respectable young lady, Lady Moorehead sometimes feels the responsibility has fallen to her."

The servant's smooth brow furrowed. "But ought that not be Lady Holling's job, being as she's the oldest?"

"One might think so, only *she* is not such a stickler as my other sister." As she bent to dig again, one of the rolled-up sleeves of her shirt unfurled. She accidentally stabbed it with the trowel, pinning the fabric to the ground.

In spite of her predicament, she laughed and yanked the linen back out of the dirt. "I suspect even Lady Holling would have objections if she got an eyeful of what I've been wearing lately. As for Lady Moorehead, it doesn't bear thinking what she would do if she saw me dressed this way. You will do me a great service, James, if you don't mention this quaint costume when my sister arrives. I would truly hate for her to hear of it."

He grinned. "Mum's the word, miss."

"I appreciate your discretion." She started to turn away, then thought twice and looked back. "James, you've been clearing out the hypocaust for hours on end. Why don't you leave off and see how our horses are faring? It's been a long day, and I expect Anima would welcome the attention."

"Yes, miss!" The wide smile he gave her showed how much he welcomed the suggestion. "Thank you."

"Thank *you*. As usual, you've been a great help to me."

A crimson tinge crept up the groom's cheeks, but his eyes sparkled. With a bob of the head, he darted away from the side of the trench.

Mellie watched him disappear behind the piles of dirt, glad that she'd given him a chance for respite. She knew the ancient villa held no real interest for him, but tending the horses gave him nothing but enjoyment.

As she refocused on retrieving the missing piece of pottery, her satisfaction faded. The cave-in had choked the tunnel with debris, all of which needed to be inspected for tiny artifacts. She stared at the rubble with reluctance, then let her tools fall at her feet. The process would take forever, and she had counted on reconstructing this pot today.

With Terry arriving on the morrow, she debated taking a shortcut in the procedure. She could scoop the loose soil to the side and sift through it later. Normally she refrained from putting off tedious work to leap ahead to the reward, but just this once would it be so bad to indulge herself?

Resolved, she retrieved her trowel and launched into a second unearthing of the shaft. She quickly found that the cave-in had altered the shape and size of the tunnel. The opening remained narrow but now stood some three feet high and sank back nearly as deep. Calculating that the piece she sought lay toward the rear of the cavity, she squeezed an arm between the walls and concentrated her efforts there.

To her surprise, she soon struck a hard protrusion she had failed to notice during the original dig. Curious, she set down her tools and reached as far as she could into the hole. Through the clumsy gardener's glove on her hand, she distinguished a long, slim form—slim enough to suggest that it was made of metal.

"A shield," she whispered. "Or a plate perhaps." Her heartbeat quickened. Most of the artifacts uncov-

ered on the villa consisted of ceramic or glass, and
they had never come across an intact piece of armor.

She attempted to move the object, but it held fast.
Pulling out her arm, she stripped away her glove and
reached back in barehanded. There it was—thin,
encrusted, and cold—a metal plate of some sort. A
characteristically bumpy surface indicated the possibility of a relief design.

"James!" She backed out and sprang to her feet.
On tiptoes, she could see slightly beyond the side of
the pit. "James!"

When the groom looked up from the horse he was
tending, she motioned for him to come to her. As soon
as she saw him wave back, she ducked down again to
stare into the tunnel.

A moment later, his voice sounded from above.
"Yes, miss?"

"Bring me a lamp, please." She spoke loudly to
counteract the muffling effect of the surrounding earth.
"I believe I left my equipment pack over by the old
oak when I stopped for lunch. Please fetch it for me."

While waiting for his return, she peered into the
blackness, but her eyes failed to adjust. She turned
sideways to try to squeeze into the tunnel, but the effort
was useless. Backing out, she knocked her hat awry
on the close walls.

James reappeared above the trench, holding the large,
lumpy satchel. He handed it down to her with a bland
expression. "Find another pot, did you?"

She looked up at his impassive face, wishing someone well versed in archaeology were present to share
in her discovery. "No, not a pot, but I believe there
may be something else here. My father could likely
tell more. Please ask him to come to me."

"Mrs. Burke just called Sir William up to the house.
Should I ride up and fetch him?"

Her excitement almost led her to say yes, but common sense made her think twice. "No, you had better not. Mrs. Burke wouldn't call for Papa unless the matter were important, and I only wanted an opinion."

As the groom waited for further instructions, she bit her lip. She could send for Bennie, but he might not appreciate being disturbed his first day back at the villa. On the other hand, the prospect of finding a Roman-era silver plate might excite him. Yes, surely it would.

She turned back to James. "Do you know if Mr. Romney is still working on the mosaic?"

"I expect he is—as well as Lord St. Leger."

"Oh, yes." She had to resist making a face at the mention of Ben's companion. The pompous coxcomb had blasted her one too many times in the past, and she planned to do all she could to avoid him during this stay. St. Leger had to lord it over everyone, merely because he was titled . . . and moneyed. Well, he was handsome, too. That likely fueled his ego further. In any case, how was she to get Bennie to come over without his insufferable friend tagging along?

"Shall I fetch them for you?" James asked.

"Well . . . see if you can get Mr. Romney." She took in a deep breath. Maybe St. Leger wouldn't bother coming over with Ben, after all. The man had made no effort to talk to her at dinner the night before. If he continued showing such disinterest in her, she'd be perfectly happy. "No need to disturb both of them. I need only one opinion."

The groom started off, and she rummaged through the equipment pack, drawing out a battered oil lamp and tinderbox. She lit the lamp and crammed it into the tight opening. Within another moment, she had abandoned all thoughts of anything but the plate.

* * *

Miles was surprised to receive a summons from his host's daughter. He swatted a wayward strand of his thick, dark brown hair out of his eyes and sat back on his haunches. What would prompt Melpomene to ask him for a consultation? He certainly hoped she wasn't sending out some sort of coquette's lure. If Bennie were around, he would have sent him to her instead. The naive fool wouldn't even have minded.

"Can Miss Lowery not wait until Mr. Romney returns from the gatehouse?" he asked her groom.

The young fellow glanced back over his shoulder, twisting his mouth in a nervous manner. "I don't believe so. She was rather anxious for someone to come to her. First she asked for her father, but he's gone up to the house, so she sent me over here."

Miles took in the fact that she had initially asked for the baronet. That seemed to indicate she had a real concern. What if she had some serious problem, and he put her off? Sir William wouldn't be too pleased with him.

He sighed and got to his feet. "Very well. Allow me to note where I'm leaving off. Then you can show me where she's working."

As he scribbled in his log, he thought back on his shock upon first seeing Miss Lowery the day before. Even more disturbing had been his reaction to her appearance last night at dinner. In a simply styled navy blue gown, she had appeared every bit as exotic as she had dressed like a hoyden. His weakness for the little minx bothered him. All evening he'd made a point of staying away from her, and he planned to do the same whenever possible in the future.

Still, as Ben had pointed out, he might be placing

too much importance on her presence. Perhaps he'd be better off getting used to the idea that she might call him over on occasion. Why should such a trivial matter bother him? Her being here meant nothing to him.

"Very well. I am right behind you," he said to her groom, stashing away his notebook. He hoisted himself out of the pit where the mosaic lay. Trailing reluctantly behind the young man, he made his way toward the east wing of the villa. Twice he stopped to knock clumps of soil from his black Hessian boots. His valet would have cringed at the neglected condition of the finely crafted footwear. Happily, he never brought the servant along during his frequent stays at archaeological sites.

When they reached the trench Miss Lowery occupied, he spotted her bending over, squeezing her head and shoulders into a cramped cavity. Her posture gave him a pronounced view of her leather-covered bottom.

He froze in place at the side of the pit. As much as he wanted to consider her presence unremarkable, those clothes she wore—especially from this perspective— could not help but affect him. Gaping, he noted to himself that she had a magnificent bottom.

Behind him, the groom snickered, and the base sound woke Miles up to his folly. A pang of annoyance usurped his stupefaction. He was hot and dusty, he had made a fool of himself in front of a stripling of a servant, and it was all the fault of a ridiculous chit who had no sense of her own femininity—or *pretended* she didn't.

"Miss Lowery!" He darted a glare back at the groom, who at once sobered and began to make his way toward two horses grazing under a tree.

Miles looked to the trench again and still found himself faced with the woman's posterior. Hands on hips, he forced his gaze to a mound of dirt several yards away from her. "Miss Lowery, I understand you require some assistance?"

"I've found something." She pulled her head out of the shaft and removed her crooked hat, dislodging a hairpin. Wine red tresses cascaded down about her face. When she met his gaze she looked oddly surprised but quickly recovered her composure. "A metal plate—possibly a silver platter with a relief."

When he only stood there, dumbfounded, her brow crinkled. "My lord?"

"Er, yes." He gathered his wits and slid down the side of the ditch, scowling over his second lapse in dignity. Besides, her speculation was ludicrous. "Silver platters were highly uncommon in Roman Britain. The artifact is far more likely to be an iron shield or a pewter plate. Where is it?"

"To the rear of this cavity." They knelt in unison, and she offered him her lamp. "There is not much to see. Your sense of touch may serve you better."

He seized the lamp and thrust it through the opening. Peering into the dimly lit cavern, he saw nothing but dirt and crumbled stone. Melpomene's arm brushed his own, and the faint scent of lavender teased his nostrils. Did the chit have to crowd him so?

"Do you see it?" Her breathless voice came from close to his ear. "A ridge projecting from the back wall."

He steered his attention to the spot she described. Yes, it did seem to be the edge of some sort of plate. Straightening up, he pulled the lamp back out. "I can't tell much from looking at it. Let me see what I can feel."

"You'll find it rather difficult to reach," she said as he leaned sideways into the hole, his face toward her, "though perhaps your longer arms will grant you more success than I had. Unfortunately, the object is lodged in there quite tightly. This whole mound will have to be excavated before we can retrieve it.'' Studying the area, she sighed. ''In fact, now that I consider it, the work is likely to go very slowly after tomorrow.''

He didn't understand what she referred to, but he wasn't about to further the conversation by asking. Straining to touch the artifact, he said, ''Well, if it sat here for some fifteen hundred years, I shouldn't think another month or so will make much difference.''

She raised her eyebrows. ''Given your great devotion to Romano-British artifacts, I am rather surprised this piece doesn't interest you more.''

He frowned. Perhaps she had a point—but he wouldn't bother telling her so.

''Is something wrong?'' she asked. ''Perhaps your work on the mosaic is not progressing swiftly enough for you?''

Was that a hint of sarcasm in her tone? He clenched his jaw, but he had to admit that the fact he'd made himself look like a simpleton in front of the groom was more his own fault than hers.

''Forgive me,'' he forced himself to say, one arm still extended in the hole. ''You've hit precisely upon the problem. I am overheated and aggravated from digging out that confounded mass of tile. I trust that you know how frustrating such a task can be.''

She shrugged. ''I can't say that I do. Archaeology intrigues *me*.''

This time he definitely detected ridicule in her voice. He let off reaching for a moment. ''You *never* grow tired on a dig?''

''Certainly not my first day at a site.'' She met his gaze with steady blue-green eyes. ''Perhaps you need some time away from the field. When one loses all sense of fascination, 'tis a sign one has been working for too long.''

Little did she know *something* had been fascinating him—something that should have held no appeal at all. He chose to ignore her advice and turned back to the article hidden in the shaft. When he got a better feel for it, he was surprised. She seemed to be right about its composition.

"This *is* a metal relief," he said. "Of course, from here there is no saying what type of metal. The surface is thoroughly encrusted. What led you to believe it might be silver?"

"I am relying on little more than a hunch." She spoke with complete self-assurance. "There is a small clear area on the surface that feels marvelously smooth, the way silver does. I imagine iron would be rather more corroded."

He could discern no clear spot on the plate. "I am afraid I shan't be able to verify your opinion, because I can barely reach it. You were squeezed into this hole farther than I can manage." He backed out and stood. "But it does look as though you have come across something unusual. Oddly enough, we are outside the villa wall. I wonder why the plate is buried here."

"The location *is* curious, since our outside finds are typically items the ancients discarded. They would not be so quick to toss aside a metal plate as they would a broken pot. But we will have no probable explanation until this whole section is laid open." She leaned forward and struggled to push a large rock in front of the opening.

"You needn't bother with that, you know," he said. Nevertheless, he bent down and took over the task. "The plate is too thoroughly entombed for anyone to get to it readily."

"I know, but I'll feel better when the opening is not

so obvious." She got up and brushed off her hands, as he slid the rock in place. "I'm going up to the house to tell Papa what we've found. Would you and Ben care to join me and hear what he has to say? It's probably about time we quit for the day, anyway."

"Ben had to go back to the gatehouse to research something."

"Oh."

Silence hung between them while he considered whether he should go with her. He didn't want to prolong his time in her company, but he was curious about what Sir William would say—and he *was* here to study the villa, wasn't he?

"I believe I shall take you up on the offer. I should like to hear your father's views."

She looked down at her feet. "Very well. I'll gather up my equipment, get my horse, and meet you by the mosaic."

Far from acting seductive, she looked almost displeased that he was accompanying her. He supposed that should have made him happy. "I'll see you there."

He hurried back to his side of the villa, redirecting his thoughts to her unusual find. It couldn't be a silver plate. The odds against such a discovery were too great. Stashing away his equipment, he left the pit and walked to his horse.

While he was mounting, Melpomene rode up beside him, her groom trailing behind her. He nodded to her and guided his horse up alongside hers. As they moved toward the house, he could think of nothing to say, but perhaps remaining silent was for the best.

"What ill luck that I should make this discovery just when my sister is expected," she said suddenly.

He nearly fell off the saddle. "I beg your pardon?"

"My sister Terry arrives tomorrow for a visit. She always was missish about my research, and now that

I am a grown woman she is certain to consider it beyond the pale. I shall be lucky to get any work done during her stay.''

A sick lump rose in his throat. He would kill Ben!

But, no, he knew his friend hadn't known about this. Sir William hadn't even mentioned it to them the day before. He supposed they'd had too much else to catch up on.

Swallowing, he asked, ''How long will she be visiting?''

''I cannot say for certain but likely not as long as she ought to. She's been rusticating in the West Indies for years, so she won't want to miss the London Season. Papa is bound to be disappointed when she goes.''

So the virago would only be here briefly—and she was married now, he reminded himself. Still trying to conceal his misgivings, he said, ''No doubt your father would prefer to have all his daughters settled close to him, but it's a fact of life that marriage comes along and sweeps a woman away from her family.''

Melpomene sniffed. ''Sometimes, perhaps, but I find it shameful that the institution should take two daughters so far away from a man who has lost his wife prematurely. I cannot believe that *both* of them traipsed off to Antigua. At least I am here for him.''

He shifted his gaze from the path to her profile. ''But you'll be marrying, too, before long.''

''No, I shan't.'' She turned to look him in the eye. ''I doubt that my priorities—that is, my father and my research—would sit well with a husband. And I am not about to change those priorities.''

He raised an eyebrow, doubting her sincerity. ''Surely you don't truly see yourself still digging up Dorset ten or twenty years from now?''

''Hardly. Within a few years, I expect to have moved on to Greece or Egypt.''

He caught a flash of a grin before she looked away and nudged her mare into a gallop. The breeze that fanned him brought with it another rush of fascination with her—though he knew she must be toying with him. The dreams she'd expressed resembled his own, but from a woman the ideas were preposterous.

Her groom flew off after her, and Miles frowned. Clearly she had that fellow in her pocket. Watching them gain distance on him and his horse, he shook his head to himself.

A hundred yards ahead, Melpomene dismounted in front of the house. The boy's breeches she wore underscored the grace of her movements. No boy dismounted with such fluid motion. Despite his doubts of her declared aspirations, a fanciful image popped into his mind: He imagined—a score of years from now and a thousand miles away—coming across that leather-clad feminine bottom again amidst some classical ruin.

He snorted over his own foolishness. Speeding up his horse, he rushed to catch up with her before she entered the house.

Three

As Mellie slid out of the saddle and turned her horse over to a footman, she heard the swelling sound of advancing hooves from behind her. Perhaps she should not have relegated the earl to riding in her wake, but an irresistible imp had taken hold of her when he began quizzing her about the future. She had seen that supercilious lift of his aristocratic nose, and she didn't care. She had no intention of stooping to the level of trying to justify herself to him.

Still excited over her discovery, she ran up the front steps of the manor. Glancing back, she saw Lord St. Leger dismounting from his massive black gelding. He tossed his reins to a footman and took the steps two at a time. Waiting no longer, she erupted into the front hall.

"Papa!" She rushed past the series of statues that lined the corridor and ducked into the second door on the left. Finding her father's private study unoccupied, she swung back out and dashed across to the library to repeat the same swift motion. That room, too, stood empty.

As she whirled back around, she nearly collided with the earl, who must have been right at her heels. He caught her by the elbows and looked down at her with chocolate brown eyes. She had never before noticed their color. He was quite tall, too, she thought, staring up at him—and his hands felt warm and strong on her arms.

He let go of her and cleared his throat. "I believe I hear voices coming from the rear of the house."

Wrenching herself out of her reverie, she looked down the hall toward a pair of heavy wooden doors. The sound of her father's booming laugh permeated them.

Brushing past St. Leger, she hurried down the hall and threw open the doors.

"Papa, you'll never believe what I . . ." She stopped in her tracks when she saw he was not alone. A woman wearing a bottle green traveling dress in the height of fashion stood before him, a matching poke bonnet in one of her gloved hands. When she turned toward the entrance, Mellie recognized her.

"Terry!" Seeing the familiar face after so many years brought an unexpected lump to her throat. She rushed forward and flung her arms around her sister, fairly crushing the elegant bonnet she carried. "You have come a day early."

Terry felt stiff in her arms. On stepping back for a better look at her, Mellie saw that the tension signified more than mere fatigue. Her normally fair complexion had taken on a scarlet hue, and her sea green eyes looked stormy as they flitted back and forth between Sir William and Lord St. Leger.

Finally Terry leaned forward and whispered, "Mellie, this is too shocking. What can you mean by allowing yourself to be seen like this?"

Her jaw dropped. She had completely forgotten her

attire. Now she looked down at the soiled shirt and breeches. "Oh, I am so sorry. I would never . . . that is, we are not at home to company today, I assure you, and we did not expect you until tomorrow, or I . . ."

"Never mind that now." Her sister strode several feet away from the rest of them, ostensibly to look out one of the many windows lining the outer wall of the room. After a moment she turned back around, fingers clenched around her bonnet. "Why don't you take a moment to show me the changes made to the Blue Salon, Mellie? I have been anxious to see the new drapes ever since you wrote me about them."

A harsh tone belied her interest, and a glance at the earl told Mellie that he, too, comprehended her sister's real motive. Her father, on the other hand, continued to beam at the sight of his reunited daughters.

"Yes, of course," she said, casting her gaze down at her feet.

"Must you run off so soon?" Sir William asked. "Miles has not even had a chance to greet you, Euterpe." He looked to the earl. "You two are acquainted, are you not?"

"We have met." St. Leger gave a slight bow. "Welcome home, ma'am."

Terry nodded but failed to muster up a smile for him. "I hope you will excuse me, sir, if I take a somewhat hasty leave of you. After my extended trip, I am afraid I'm not quite equal to receiving company."

"I understand perfectly." He gave her a bland look, but Mellie sensed he was annoyed.

Unconcerned, Terry walked to a nearby chair where her reticule rested.

For once embarrassed by her sister's behavior, instead of the other way around, Mellie looked toward the earl. When he met her gaze, however, she looked away. What did she care about sparing the feelings of an arrogant oaf like him?

"I am afraid I must object to your last sentiment, Euterpe." Sir William took a draw on his pipe. "Here at Lowery Park, we like to think of our visiting scholars as part of the family. After all, Miles and Ben will be here all summer. They're spending more time with us than most young men do with their families. I flatter myself to believe they will join me in urging you not to stand on ceremony with them."

When he looked expectantly toward the earl, St. Leger murmured an ambiguous assent.

Terry let out an exasperated sigh. "I am certain that once I settle in I shall be pleased to comply with your wishes, Papa. However, I hope it is not overnice in a woman who has barely completed a long journey to want to freshen up before socializing, even with her family."

He chuckled. "You do as you feel fit, my dear. I cannot pretend to comprehend all of the niceties a lady's sensibilities dictate, can I?"

She looked from her father to Mellie, her lips pressed into a tight line. "I rather think not."

Again, Mellie regretted her sister's lack of breeding. She avoided looking at St. Leger, unwilling to see the certain disapproval in his face.

Surprisingly, Terry went to her father and kissed his brow. "We shall see you shortly, Papa, after we have changed for tea. Come along, Melpomene." Dropping a brief curtsy toward her father's guest, she swept toward the door.

"Yes, ma'am." Mellie started to follow her out of the room, then she remembered why she'd come up to the house. Turning to face the earl, she said, "Miles, can you hold off on saying anything about the . . . about what we . . ." Her words failed her once she

realized she had addressed him in the familiar manner
of her father.

His lips twitched, though he didn't grin outright.
"Certainly, that can wait. You had better go on now."

She gave him a nod and left the room, mortified by
the whole scene, though she told herself she shouldn't
have cared. What St. Leger thought of her family didn't
matter, nor did what Terry thought of her.

Nevertheless, she followed her sister into the Blue
Salon. Terry closed the tall French doors behind them,
took a deep breath and turned to face her.

Mellie crossed her arms over her chest, prepared for
the upbraiding she knew was coming.

"Melpomene," Terry said, "I parted from my husband while he went on to York solely because I could
not wait to return to the bosom of my family. The last
way I want to start off my visit is with a lecture to my
fully grown sister, but this . . . *this!*" She broke off
with a gesture toward Mellie's clothing.

Mellie sighed, annoyed to be once again cast in the
role of naughty child. Terry had always had a knack
for belittling her, but she had hoped four years apart
from one another would make a difference in their
relationship. "Believe me, this is a highly unusual case.
I would not normally—"

"Highly unusual?" She let out a humorless laugh.
"You need not tell *me* so. I cannot fathom how you
could do this to yourself and to the respectability of
your family. Perhaps Father is too eccentric to see any
harm in your dressing so disgracefully, but anyone
with half a sense of propriety . . ." She trailed off and
turned her back.

Mellie stepped around her sister's shoulder in order
to face her again. "Believe me, this is also the last
way I wanted to greet you, but you must understand
that even I rarely take *deshabille* to such lengths as I

have today. When I am digging, I usually wear an old morning gown or the like, but I wanted to work quickly before your visit, and this attire makes movement easier. I had actually hoped to spare you from encountering what I knew you'd view as unladylike behavior. Unfortunately, my plan went awry.''

Terry's face remained grim. ''I am afraid your priorities are misplaced, Melpomene. *I* am not the one you have 'to spare,' as you put it. There have been many times when I have seen you in less than a pair of boy's breeches, and so long as you are dressed so within the confines of your own chamber, it does not signify. But to come marching into the main parlor with nary a thought as to who might be present . . . Nay, why should you have given it a thought, considering in whose company you were already?''

Mellie gritted her teeth. To argue seemed a shame when the two of them had not seen each other in years, but she refused to submit completely to her sister's remonstrances. ''As Papa told you, Miles is practically one of the family. You may not be able to see that from your position outside the household.''

''I cannot imagine appearing before even a *real* brother looking as you do, let alone in front of someone 'practically' family—especially when that person happens to be one of the most eligible bachelors in the kingdom.''

Despite her vexation, Mellie choked back a laugh. Terry sounded exactly like one of those matchmaking mothers who paraded their daughters around London. '' 'One of the most eligible bachelors in the kingdom'? Is that how you think of him?''

Her sister showed no sign of humor. ''And how do you think of the man?''

''The way everyone here does. I respect him as an accomplished scholar and as a guest of Papa's. I certainly would never view him as merchandise on the marriage mart." The thought of any woman pursuing that pompous oaf made her laugh outright.

"You may find that description humorous, my dear, but I assure you that any *normal* young woman would not be so surprised. The man's good looks are apparent enough, even when he is as disheveled as he was today. And I don't suppose you could be ignorant of the fact that he is sole heir to an elderly uncle with a weighty title."

"Ah, but that is where you are mistaken." Mellie held up her index finger in the manner of an exacting governess refuting an incorrect quiz answer. "*I* can only suppose that in your long absence from our homeland you *are* ignorant of the fact that he inherited that title some time ago." She let a broad grin spread across her face.

Terry looked heavenward before meeting her gaze again. "So you dress like a hoyden before a peer of the realm and then you make light of it? This is beyond everything. How old are you now—nearly two-and-twenty? At your age you ought to take some measure of interest in your future. Lord St. Leger, as I shall now properly refer to the man you would adopt as a brother, has command of one of the largest estates in England."

Mellie raised a hand to her mouth in feigned surprise. "Perhaps in the world, for that matter. But surely you recall that I am well enough provided for, whether or not I marry. I have no need to be vulgarly sniffing out a fortune among my male acquaintances."

"No, you don't, but perhaps you should be 'sniffing out' a life with one of them. Do you truly want to spend the better part of your existence alone in the world? Naturally, you will always have Clio's family and mine, but that is not quite the same as having your own. None of us can change the fact that Father is getting on in years and will not be around forever. You have always had him to pamper you. Who will pamper you when he is gone?''

The amusement Mellie felt drained, resurfacing as anger. ''I need no one to pamper me. And how dare you speak that way about Papa? Perhaps you don't realize it, being away for so long, but our father is in perfect health. He will be with us for many years to come.''

A sudden change came over Terry. The hard lines of resentment around her mouth melted, and her brow creased with concern. She stepped forward and put her arm around Mellie. ''I'm sorry, love. I never meant to upset you. I am only worried about your future.''

Mellie leaned into her shoulder, ready to be placated the minute Terry gave her the chance. She would never admit it, but she often missed her sisters. Though she had spent her youth rejecting practically everything they embraced, she'd lately come to wonder if resentment for their assumed authority over her had sometimes made her stubborn.

''Have you never thought about a husband?'' Terry asked.

In truth, she had given more thought to marriage than she cared to say. A year or so ago, she had nursed a secret *tendre* for the vicar's younger brother, Mr. Thomas Dowden, whose sandy curls and lush lips reminded her of a Greek statue. She had looked forward to his visits to the vicarage and made many attempts to speak to him after church.

Eventually, however, the snatches of conversation she had culled from him led her to fear he might have little more in his head than a Greek statue. Then, a summer ago, he had married the most scatterbrained bit of fluff in the village, confirming her worst suspi-

cions. The experience had caused her a great deal of
pain—but, of course, she had since developed a more
mature view of marriage.

"I have thought about it," she confessed. "But there
is my work to take into account. I should not want
anyone interfering with my research."

"Your research?" Terry's lips formed a grim line.
She took a deep breath and sighed. "Well, who says
you cannot continue your research while you look
around a bit? One activity need not preclude the other.
And, you know, now is the time to do it. You are a
lovely young lady, but the bloom of youth always
helps, and it does not last forever."

Mellie forced herself to hold back a retort. At least
her sister hadn't argued about her work. "Can we
perhaps speak about this another time? You've barely
set foot in the house."

Terry hesitated, then gave her a last hug and released
her. "I suppose so. However, I do have one last thought
I want to put in your head. Keep in mind that I'm not
looking for a reaction from you now. Promise me you'll
give the idea some consideration before you reject it."

"Sounds promising," Mellie muttered.

Her sister ignored her. "You know how much I love
the London Season. Well, Moorehead will be busy up
north until June, and by the time he gets here I will
have missed another spring in town. What I propose
is that you and I set up house in London for a month
or two. We would have such great fun."

"For a month or two?" Mellie blinked at her. "I
could not possibly leave Father—"

"Now, now. You promised you'd give the idea some
thought."

Of course she hadn't promised, but she'd already
had enough arguing for one day. She tried to think of
a compromise. "Perhaps I could *visit* you for a few

days—or maybe come with you for a week and help
you get settled. By then you'll be in touch with all of
your old friends again, and I can return to Papa.''

"Don't be a peagoose. Father can spare you far
longer than a sennight." She tapped a finger on her
chin. "Six weeks should be quite enough."

"Enough for what?"

"For me to introduce you about. I shall not plan a
ball or anything extravagant, mind you, for I know
how little that sort of thing would appeal to you."

Mellie gaped at her. "Do you?"

Terry began pacing the floor. "We need only attend
a few routs, perhaps have a dinner party or two, and
go to some of the more desirable balls. Of course, I'll
have to see about getting you vouchers to Almack's.
I daresay that Clio and I married well enough that
being our sister can do you no disservice."

Mellie felt as though she were going to explode—
then it occurred to her that her father would never go
along with such a plan. He tended to be overprotective
of her, as the youngest child, and he'd never before
let her go away without him. She took care how to
phrase her reply. "I feel sure it cannot, and I do appreciate your offer. All I can say is that I shall leave it to
Papa's discretion."

"Wonderful." Terry beamed at her. "You'll take
well, I think. You're quite the most handsome of us
Lowery girls, if only you would not take such pains
to hide your beauty. Now don't you worry about Papa.
I know you are sometimes a bit oversensitive about
him, but I shall choose just the right moment and
present the idea to him in a very positive light."

Mellie nodded.

"I don't feel we should broach the subject tonight.
I shouldn't want him to think I'm eager to leave his
house the moment I step inside."

She frowned. "I should hope *not.*"

"I'm glad you concur. Now let us get you out of that atrocity and into something civilized. Meanwhile, I will tell you all about how dear Clio and her boys are doing . . . and Holling and Moorehead, too."

Relieved to drop the topic, Mellie took the arm her sister proffered. She left the room in relative peace, satisfied she'd hear little or nothing more about her going to London.

Four

Mellie sat with her father and sister before the big stone fireplace in the main parlor of the manor. All during dinner and for an hour since then, Terry had been regaling her and Papa with dozens of anecdotes about life in the West Indies. To her, the most entertaining stories were the ones about Clio's young sons. Simply being able to ask questions about their growth and accomplishments was a treat.

"You say young Will is now nearly as tall as his mother?" Sir William leaned forward in his favorite armchair, hanging on Terry's every word. "I find it hard to credit."

" 'Tis true, Papa," she said, eyes shining. "The boy obviously takes after Holling in that respect, for you know how petite our Clio is. Everyone agrees that he's likely to surpass her height within the year."

Sir William shook his head, though his face registered approval. "And little Robin, is he as hale and hearty as his brother?"

"Oh Lord, yes." Terry lifted a glass of orgeat and took a sip. "I believe Robin will prove the one who most emulates you. He began study with a tutor only this past autumn, but by all accounts his progress is outstanding."

While the proud grandfather inquired into particulars, Mellie shifted positions on a stiff-backed settee. Both the seat and the warmth of the fire were beginning to bother her, but the conversation, too, had a drawback to it. Though she treasured this chance to learn about her sisters' families, it distressed her to realize how rapidly their lives were passing by without her. She let out a sigh. "By the time we see the boys again, they'll be full-grown men."

Terry paused to pour herself another drink from a crystal decanter. "La, Mellie, they'll be back in England before you know it. Clio and Holling have been speaking of their return for ages. I shouldn't be surprised if Moorehead's and my departure sets a fire under them at last."

"Then you don't think Holling might be tempted to stay on in Antigua indefinitely?" Sir William asked, his gaze searching hers. "They've been gone so long that I'd begun to fear as much. Does he trust the plantation manager enough to leave the operation in the fellow's hands?"

"Undoubtedly." Terry held her glass up to a candle and studied the syrupy liquid. "The business practically runs itself now—and with such success that Clio will live in fine style when she returns to England. The whole venture has been quite a boon to us."

"Perhaps not to Papa and me, however." With tightened lips, Mellie pushed a cream-colored cashmere shawl off her shoulders to relieve the heat. The shortsleeved dark blue cambric gown beneath sported simple styling, as fashion plates didn't number among her areas of study. "With both of you gone, not a day has passed that we haven't yearned for your company."

Terry set down her glass and gave her a crooked smile. "Things would have been much worse if only one of us had gone. Imagine how worried you would have been then. Luckily for us all, Moorehead and Holling took on the plantation together."

Sir William nodded, reaching to retrieve his pipe from a low Queen Anne table beside his chair. "And we are luckier still that you've been prosperous. Moorehead's father was such an old reprobate that he left little but debts to your husband. I confess that when you and he married I had some doubts as to how you would live, but that makes it all the sweeter to hear of your success now."

Mellie could not quite justify the loss of her sisters' companionship in exchange for their monetary gain, but to say so would only stir up a hornet's nest. Instead, she judged she had allowed Terry enough time in the limelight that she could bring up the subject she'd been waiting to broach all evening. "Speaking of success, Papa, I've been wanting to tell you what I came across at the villa today."

In the midst of refilling his pipe, Sir William did not look up to answer. "Oh, love, why don't we talk of the villa another time? You know Terry is not interested in dirt and pottery, and she still has a great deal to tell us about Antigua."

Mellie blinked at him, not used to being rebuffed by her father. She took a moment to form her objection. "But this may be an extraordinary find. Lord St. Leger and I came up to the house this afternoon expressly to tell you about it, but we never got the chance."

He touched a flaming lucifer to his tobacco and turned to face Terry. "How do you feel about it, dear? I'm sure you'd prefer to continue our conversation about the West Indies, and you *are* our guest tonight."

She let out a tinkling laugh. "Is that not a strange

thought? I, a guest at Lowery Park. If I were to claim that privilege, what I should truly like to hear is all of the local gossip. However, since I'm aware how unsuited you two are to speak on that topic, we may as well listen to what my sister has to say.''

Mellie needed no further invitation. ''I've found a silver plate.'' Flushed with pent-up excitement, she stood and moved into the cooler space behind her seat. ''That is, I believe I have. While clearing a narrow tunnel outside the east wall, I stumbled onto a metal object projecting from the rear. The surface is bumpy to the touch, as though embellished with a relief, but I could make out nothing visually. I'll need to do quite a bit more digging before I can confirm my impression.''

Sir William regarded her with a creased brow. ''I don't want to disappoint you, my dear, but your discovery is likely to amount to nothing more than an iron shield. And if the original owners had reason to toss it out of the villa, that doesn't bode well for its condition.''

She lifted her chin. Was she imagining things, or did her father seem oddly unreceptive to her lately? ''I realize that could be the case, but my instincts lead me to think otherwise. And St. Leger seemed to find the discovery promising.''

''Miles examined the object, as well? And he also judged the composition to be silver?''

''Well . . . he didn't precisely say so, but he showed considerable interest in the find.''

''He would, would he not?'' Terry balanced her drink in one hand, rearranging the folds of her burnt orange organza gown with the other. ''I take it that Lord St. Leger is just as intrigued by Roman ruins as you two are. Why else would he be living in a dilapidated gatehouse when he owns a beautiful abbey, situated as near as Devonshire?''

"I shouldn't call the gatehouse dilapidated," Sir William said, though he did not appear offended. "Clearly, a mere cottage is no match for *any* of Miles' own properties, but as a dedicated scholar he's unlikely to mind doing without a few luxuries. I'm pleased that he's come here to study again. It shows he considers the villa a worthy site."

"Yes, I understand that the Park is rich with relics." Terry leaned her elbow on the armrest and set her chin in her hand. "Remember the little stone statue I once found on the way to Gough Lodge? Lord, I loved going to visit the Goughs when I was a girl. At the height of my friendship with Gwyneth, I called on her so often I might as well have resided there. I wonder how often she returns to visit the Lodge these days."

The baronet contemplated a swirl of smoke that floated above his head. "Didn't the old viscount and his wife both die years ago? Your friend's brother must have inherited at that time, but I've heard nothing of the family in ages."

Mellie could scarcely believe that her father had taken so little notice of her discovery. True, her sister had been away from home for years, but Terry had been talking about her own concerns for hours. Any other evening Mellie and Sir William would have sat and conferred about the villa without fatigue. She knew she couldn't expect quite the same attention with Terry home, but she never dreamed she would be ignored.

She bent over and scooped up her shawl from the settee. "I believe I'll step outside and take in some air. The atmosphere in here has become monstrously stuffy."

Sir William gave an indifferent nod, and Terry barely paused between sentences.

Mellie flung her wrap around her shoulders and stalked out of the room. Dashing past the staring statues in the hall, she fled through the front door. She stepped to the edge of the portico and gulped in the brisk night air. Something strange was going on with Papa. His behavior wasn't due only to Terry's visit. Now that she thought back, several times in the last month or so, she had noticed an unusual reticence in him.

What could be the matter? Was he tired of the villa? Was Terry right about him getting older? Archaeology could be a toilsome pursuit. Perhaps he could no longer do it.

Swallowing, she descended the steps and crossed the gravel drive to the grass, the dew cool on her sandaled feet. She would have to ask him, of course, as soon as they had a moment alone . . . and as soon as she could get his attention.

That was the most disturbing aspect of all of this— that he'd seemed so warm toward Terry but reserved with *her*. Could it possibly be that his unease had something to do with her?

Within the snug study of the gatehouse, the sound of a low snore prompted Miles to look up from the massive mahogany escritoire. As he suspected, Ben's tousled blond head had drooped to the arm of the sofa. A London newspaper lay abandoned on his narrow chest, fluttering faintly with each shallow breath he expelled.

Miles glanced up at the clock on the mantel and found it had just gone eight. Sighing, he set the quill pen he'd been using into a silver holder. He shoved a pile of archaeological notes to the side, rose, and moved in front of the senseless figure. "I realize we keep country hours here, but is this not taking it too far, Ben?"

His friend responded by stirring and knocking the newspaper to the floor. Then he snored again.

Miles stooped and gathered up the scattered pages from the thick Axminster carpet. Truth be told, he could understand Ben's loss of consciousness; he, too, was bored witless.

He folded the paper and placed it on the desk. Usually when he stayed at a site, a quiet life suited him well, but tonight, for some reason, he itched for diversion. That afternoon he had declined Sir William's invitation to dinner, insisting the man needed time to catch up with his daughter—but with Ben asleep, the gatehouse felt rather isolated. If he hadn't found Euterpe quite so repugnant, he might even have been tempted to walk up to the manor.

Going to the window, he spread the antiquated brown velvet drapes and gazed up at the big house. The moon shone on the marble columns, and the warm glow of candles peeped through the windows like a beacon. He wanted nothing to do, however, with Euterpe or her hoydenish sister.

The thought of Melpomene brought to mind the discovery she'd made that afternoon. By this time she must have told her father about the supposed silver plate. He wondered what the baronet had thought of the find—but, naturally, he wasn't curious enough to venture up to the house. Sir William would likely stop by the mosaic tomorrow, and he could inquire then.

He let the curtains drop and looked back to his companion. Ben grunted and pulled his feet up on the couch, turning onto his side. He looked content enough to remain here all night . . . but Miles was not.

Perhaps he'd take a walk around the grounds.

He grabbed his waistcoat and jacket from the back of a chair and slid his arms into them. Snuffing all but one candle in the room, he stole out the door and left

Ben to his dreams. He cut through the kitchen and out the back entrance.

The chill of the air and the chirping of crickets invigorated him. Yes, getting out of the gatehouse had been a good idea. Turning up the gravel drive that led toward the big house, he set off with a heightened awareness of open space and freedom. He looked up at the glittering clear sky and felt alive again.

"My lord?" A quiet feminine voice sounded over the chorus of insects.

He pulled his gaze down and could just make out a slim silhouette approaching him on the path.

"Is that you, Lord St. Leger?"

Melpomene. She stepped out of the shadows, and he could see her face, pale in the moonlight, her expression wary. It was good to see the chit lose her usual air of complete confidence once in a while, as she had that afternoon with her sister hounding her. With amusement, he remembered her embarrassment when she'd slipped and called him by his given name.

"Why such formality?" Stopping when he reached her, he tried to stifle a grin. "You called me *Miles* this afternoon."

She blinked at him, then looked off into the woods. "Did I? I apologize. I must have acquired that familiarity from my father. As you heard, he insists that we consider you part of the family."

He studied her profile, admiring the small, straight nose. When his gaze dropped to her lips, the urge he got to kiss her startled him. What the devil was he thinking? Scrambling to recover his wits, he cleared his throat. "Very flattering, I'm sure. Your father is an accommodating host, as well as an esteemed scholar."

She turned to face him, her expression softening. "Thank you."

" 'Tis only the truth."

"Papa will bend over backward to indulge the people he cares about." She bit her lip. "I suppose you're right about the name question. Bennie calls me Mellie. You should, too."

"Oh." The fact struck him that he'd just encouraged greater intimacy between them. How stupid could he be? But now that it was done, he couldn't very well backtrack. "Thank you . . . Mellie."

She glanced around them. "Were you coming up to the house?"

"Er, no, just taking a late stroll." Belatedly, he wondered why she was out here alone. A pang of paranoia made him suspect she'd somehow known he would be here—but he realized she couldn't have. "What about you?"

"The same."

They glanced at each other for an uncomfortable instant. He wondered whether he could concoct a reason to continue on his separate way, but to leave a woman walking in the dark alone was unconscionable.

"What is the best path for nighttime walking?" he asked.

She hesitated, then nodded in the direction he'd come from. "Come this way."

They turned down a side path he hadn't noticed before. The dirt trail narrowed, and he had to move behind her.

"Isn't this a bit overgrown for walking in the dark?" he asked.

"Only for a moment, then it comes out by the stream."

He followed her, and they emerged beside a creek that ran through the middle of the estate. She turned to walk alongside the water. Reluctantly, he stepped up beside her. *This is where she'll muster up her seductive arts,* he thought. He would simply have to end this walk before she could put him and herself in an embarrassing situation by forcing him to spurn her.

"I have only a few minutes before I have to get back to the gatehouse," he said. "I left Bennie asleep in the study, and I don't want to leave the candle unattended for long."

"Oh, very well." She surprised him by giving him a faint smile. "There's a bridge around the next bend. We'll cross it and follow the other side of the stream back to the main house. Then you can head back."

"Excellent." He quickened his pace slightly. "Are you and your father enjoying catching up with your sister?"

She drew in a long breath. "For the most part."

It was a cryptic comment, but it wasn't his place to question her about it. Judging by the scene between the two women earlier, he supposed Euterpe had been scolding her—and rightly so, by his estimation. "Who is it that your sister wed? I didn't catch her married name."

"Papa would have you call her Terry, anyway—but *she* might prefer Lady Moorehead. She married Edward Haverford, Marquess Moorehead. The family is from York."

He placed the name with a middle-aged country gentleman he'd met in town once or twice years ago. "Ah, yes. Moorehead—a quiet fellow, I think."

"Mmhmm." She stared ahead at the path, not flirting with him at all—not even walking close to him. Something seemed to preoccupy her.

He noticed a bridge beside them. "Is this where we're meant to cross?"

"Sorry? Oh, yes. Forgive me, I was woolgathering."

As they turned onto the bridge, he recalled her find again. "Have you had a chance to tell Sir William about the metal plate?"

"Yes." She shook her head. "But if you wanted to hear what he had to say, I fear I shall have to disappoint you. He was so engrossed by Terry's tales of Antigua that he had no time for talk of the villa."

The news surprised him, but Sir William *had* been separated from Euterpe for years. "Likely he'll come by the east wall tomorrow to inspect the site himself. I'd wager that were this not Lady Moorehead's first night at the Park, he'd be out there with a lantern now."

Her gaze remained fixed on the darkened landscape. "I don't know. He seems to be of the opinion that the article is nothing but a discarded shield after all."

"The odds do favor a shield."

He heard her sigh just as a breeze carried her faint lavender scent to his nose. Perhaps the feminine fragrance lent her an air of vulnerability that he didn't usually sense in her. He felt a pang of sympathy over her disappointment. "At least we know it has a well preserved relief. I felt the same protuberances you described."

Her gaze shot to his. "So you're convinced about the relief? I'm glad to hear you say so. My father's attitude shook me so much I'd begun to doubt myself."

The moonlight made her eyes appear large and guileless—not necessarily an accurate reflection of her character, he reminded himself. He couldn't seem to get the scent of lavender out of his nose. Her arm brushed his, and he realized they'd drawn closer to each other. He stepped away.

"We'll only know for sure when the area is cleared." Staring ahead, he spotted the manor through a clearing in the trees and felt a wave of relief. "How did you notice the object anyway? It's lodged so far back in that hole."

She hesitated. "I'd been gathering pot shards from a tunnel in that area, and I had a little cave-in."

He shot her a look. "You didn't brace the shaft properly, did you?"

"I was in a hurry with Terry due to arrive. Normally, I do everything by the book."

He frowned, highly skeptical. Her carelessness was evident in everything she did. Such a bumbling dilettante truly didn't deserve to be working on a fine site like this.

"She doesn't approve of my work," she went on, clearly trying to defend herself. "She does all she can to discourage me. Today she had the most absurd idea yet. She actually wants me to spend the Season in town with her—two months cooped up in London. She thinks I should have a debut. As I've told you, I've no use for husband hunting."

His ears perked up. The suggestion certainly suited *him*. He'd love to have her out of his sight and out of mind. Pretending to accept her unlikely declarations that she would never wed, he asked, "But aren't there antiquities in London you'd like to see? If you went, I could recommend several fine museums and many private collections. There is a wealth of scholarly resources in the city."

She shrugged. "I suppose you have a point, in one respect. I haven't been to town since I was a child. But if I were going, I would definitely go during winter, when we can't dig here."

"This is a far safer time of year for travel. Your father would be less worried about you."

"But that's another consideration: Papa couldn't spare me for such a length of time. He's never even allowed me to travel without him. If Terry thinks he'll agree to my spending two months away from home, she's going to be sorely disappointed."

Recalling Sir William's concerns about his daughter's social life, Miles rather thought Mellie was the one in for a surprise.

He didn't know how to respond without giving away his hopes that she'd be persuaded to go. Fortunately, they had reached the portico, and he was able to bid her good night.

Walking back to the gatehouse, he felt another swell of relief. He had made it through the isolated walk with Melpomene without her trying to put him in a compromising position—or he her, for that matter. In addition, it sounded as though her sister would have her out of his hair soon. Once Mellie was gone, he'd be able to concentrate fully on the archaeological opportunities at hand.

Ironically, Euterpe might redeem this visit to Lowery Park for him, rather than ruin it, as she had last time.

Five

"My, but you look lovely today, Euterpe." Sir William paused in stirring his tea as his middle daughter made a belated arrival at breakfast. "Not everyone can look so well first thing in the morning."

Seated beside him at the table, Mellie lifted her gaze from a dish of strawberries and cream. Her sister's entrance vexed her. She'd hoped to spend some time alone with her father now, and he, too, had just come downstairs.

"And not everyone can call *this* first thing in the morning," she muttered.

"Why, thank you, Father." Terry picked up a plate at the sideboard and slid Mellie a glance. "Pray forgive any inconvenience I've caused you. I confess I took a little extra time with my toilette today."

"None worth mentioning, I'm sure," Sir William said. "Mellie and I don't normally eat much earlier than this, anyway. Besides, seeing you in such fine fettle makes up for any trifling delay. One would never believe you've spent the past month traveling."

She grinned. "La, I had no choice but to look well

today. I intend to call on a few of our neighbors, and it wouldn't do to look shabby for their first sight of me in years."

Mellie grimaced but bit back further comment.

Bringing an assortment of rolls to the table, Terry took a seat across from her. "I hope I haven't spoiled your morning plans, Mellie."

"Not at all. I've already been to the villa to set up for the day." She waited for a barrage of disapproval.

Her sister's face revealed nothing as she poured herself a steaming cup of coffee. "Ah, I thought I detected a hint of the stables amidst all the wonderful aromas of Cook's breakfast selections."

Sir William sipped his tea, apparently oblivious to the hostile undercurrents. "I'm surprised to hear that you mean to dig today, Mellie. Judging by your dress, I thought you might be making calls with Euterpe."

Caught with her mouth full, she looked down at her faded sprigged muslin gown. The frock was the least worn of the old apparel she used for digging, but worthy of no other activity.

Before she could frame a reply, Terry answered for her. "Oh no, Father. Mellie and I agree that she should continue her archaeological quest during my stay. I shouldn't want to hinder the important discovery she may be about to make."

He cocked an eyebrow. "Forgive me for saying so, dear, but is that not rather a profound change of attitude for you? In the past, you've never encouraged her digging."

"Perhaps, but I'm not quite so narrow-minded as I used to be." She looked to her sister, perhaps for affirmation, but Mellie only spooned another strawberry into her mouth. "I daresay I've grown up during my time away."

Sir William chuckled. "Do you mean to tell me

there's yet hope that I may have raised one sensible child?''

Terry opened her mouth in feigned shock. ''Oh, honestly, Father, you do my sisters and me a grave injustice. Lest I be remiss, too, allow me to note that Mellie has been just as understanding about *my* priorities.''

Mellie stopped with her spoon in the air, praying that Terry didn't mean to bring up London so soon. Papa would be so upset to learn that she was already thinking about leaving the Park.

Her father turned to her. ''Goodness, I never thought to see so much harmony under this roof. What is it that *you* have been tolerating, dear?''

''I've no idea what she means.'' She flashed her sister a warning look and searched her mind for a feasible prevarication. ''I suppose she must be referring to my promise not to wear breeches anymore.''

He laughed. ''Well, well, well. That's quite a concession, but I rather think it a good idea at your age. I applaud the decision.''

Now she would actually have to make the sacrifice. She tried not to show her disgust with herself. Forcing a nod of acknowledgment, she reached for her orange juice.

'' 'Tis indeed a commendable step, but it's not the matter I had in mind,'' Terry said, then looked at their father. ''She's all in a pother about something we have to tell you, Papa, but I assure you she has no grounds for anxiety.''

Mellie almost choked on her juice. So, she did mean to broach the subject. How could her own sister have such poor judgment?

''Allow me to take the initiative and put her out of her misery,'' Terry continued before she could regain speech. ''Now, Father, our little design may not entirely please you at first, but upon consideration I believe you'll come to see things as I do. The crux of the matter is that we plan to go to London for the Season.''

"London?" His cup landed hard on the saucer. "You mean to leave Lowery Park when you've only just arrived? Euterpe, after so long without your company, I'd hoped to have you with me for at least a good month."

Despite a sickening lump in her throat, Mellie downed the contents of her mouth. "Of course you did, Papa, and Terry cannot be in any great hurry to go. Besides, I've told her you could never spare me for more than a week. Nay, if it's too much for you to part with me at all, I simply shan't go. I'm certain she'll understand."

Terry leaned across the table and took her father's hand. "Indeed I would, sir, but before you speak, please give the matter some thought. For me, of course, this trip would mean reentry into English society. But, more importantly, it would give Mellie a chance to make her town debut—something she ought to have done years ago. Moreover, London isn't so far off that you couldn't drive in to see us, perhaps even stay for part of the Season, if you please."

He studied her face while Mellie wondered why he should be slow in expressing his reservations. When she saw him finally nod to her sister, she could only stare in disbelief.

"As little as I may care to admit it, you have several good points. I'm only too aware that I've been remiss about my youngest daughter's come-out."

Mellie's spoon slipped from her fingers and clattered on the table. Since when did her father care whether or not she made a come-out? Though her mouth now held nothing, she gulped again. "Then you will have me go . . . for a week?"

"If I followed nothing but my own whim, then, yes, that's the longest I'd part with you. Unfortunately, I don't think a week will be sufficient for our purposes." He turned to her sister. "How long do you foresee requiring, dear?"

"Clio and I each had a full six weeks for our presentations. I see no reason that Mellie shouldn't do nicely in the same amount of time."

Mellie looked back and forth between them, scarcely able to credit what she was hearing. "But, Terry, what need can *I* possibly have for a full London Season? I'm very different from you and Clio. All that socializing will only be a trial for me."

Sir William reached over and patted her shoulder. "I'm sure your sister's well aware of your character. She won't expect you to submit to more than you can shoulder."

Terry sipped her coffee. "Of course not. As I told you yesterday, I don't exactly expect to present you at court."

"Not with the circles we move in." Her father laughed and dabbed at his moustache with a napkin. "Come now, Mellie, this is something you should look forward to, not protest. I'll come to London to visit you sometime during your stay. If an old man can make the effort, it should be nothing to you."

Her face grew hot with suppressed emotion. "But what of my work? I have the plate to excavate now— possibly a major find. Nothing town has to offer could possibly be as important."

He shook his head. "Getting you settled is very important."

She could only stare. He had never before spoken of getting her settled. She'd always assumed he pictured her future much the way she did.

"You haven't been in London since my last Season,

dear,'' Terry said. "I vow you'll find a great deal more to excite you there now than when you were fifteen. Everything will be open to you. You may even be permitted to waltz, if I can pull a few strings with Almack's patronesses.''

"Permitted to waltz?'' Mellie shoved her plate to the center of the table. "What do I care for waltzing?''

Her father frowned. "Such an objection only serves to prove your sister's point, love. A young woman *ought* to care something about dancing.''

"There is more to life than dancing.'' She jumped to her feet, her chair screeching across the wooden floor. "My ballroom experience may be limited to a few country reels, but that hardly makes me unaccomplished.''

"No one would dare call you that, dear.'' Terry picked up her butter knife. "But, take it from me, never having waltzed is a shocking omission in a young life. You'll agree with me soon enough.''

"I'm willing to wager otherwise.''

Sir William rose now, too, his mouth set in a hard line. "That's quite enough arguing, Mellie. There are few times when I see fit to contest you, but I fear this is one of them.''

Appalled at the rare admonition, she could do nothing but retreat. She lowered her face and battled a nagging sense of injustice. "I'm sorry, Papa. If you truly believe a London Season would be best for me, then I must go . . . It only seems too bad about my plate.''

"The timing may be unfortunate, but putting off your trip would mean missing part of the Season. Your work will wait for you, whereas the London hostesses will not.''

She turned around and gazed out a window toward the ruins across the fields. "So I can expect six weeks of delay for the project and probably several more before the plate is uncovered. Until then, I'll simply have to wonder whether I've stumbled across a magnificent find or nothing.''

Her father drew in a ragged breath. "I realize this find means a lot to you. I've been in similar situations myself. Perhaps Ben and Miles can do something to help while you're away. If they sort through some of the rubble on top, you'll reach the artifact sooner when you return."

"But it's *my* find." She spun around to face him. "Even if they'd agree to such a plan—which I doubt— they certainly wouldn't want to leave off in the middle and wait weeks for me to come home. Can't you give me a little leeway—perhaps just a fortnight—to try to complete the work before I go? Surely you'll want to spend more time with Terry before you part with her again."

He hesitated, then looked at her sister. "Do you think you can afford to miss the beginning of the Season?"

She munched on a croissant, hardly looking concerned. "Maybe the first week, but I don't know about two. It would mean losing a good many opportunities."

Mellie shook her head. "A week will never be long enough."

Sir William held up his hands. "We shall say two at the longest, and you must do all you can to keep it to one. What's more, if I see any sign of dallying, I'll send you straight into town without delay. I'll also expect you to take full advantage of any assistance you can muster."

"What sort of assistance? Do you mean I should have James do some of the more detailed work? I'm not certain I feel comfortable with that."

"What about Ben?"

"Bennie is engrossed in the mosaic. I wouldn't dare ask him to help me."

"Then I'll ask Miles," her father said firmly. "You told me he seemed interested in your project."

She frowned. Working with St. Leger was the last thing she wanted. When she'd met him in the Park the night before, it was the first time he had behaved with more than the merest civility toward her. In the field, he'd always been especially supercilious. Even yesterday afternoon had been no exception.

"That Friday face won't get you your way this time, Melpomene." Her father gave her a look so stern it astonished her. "I ask very little of you. For once, you will have to answer to someone other than yourself."

Her jaw dropped. What had happened to her indulgent papa? In his current state, she didn't dare question him, but before she could respond at all he tossed down his napkin and strode from the room.

She turned to her sister, who looked rather surprised herself. "What on earth has come over Papa?"

Terry shrugged. "I don't know. Believe me, I didn't mean for him to ring a peal over you. I've never seen him quite so severe, even with Clio—and you know he was always most strict with her, as the eldest of us."

Mellie collapsed back into her chair and buried her face in her hands. She didn't know whether to rail at her sister or dissolve into tears. Between her father's strange behavior and her frustration with his edict, her whole body was shaking.

"Do you realize how much I dread undertaking this Season, Terry?" she asked at last.

A moment passed before her sister answered softly. "I'll do all I can to make it enjoyable for you, love . . . but, whether it is or not, you must make your debut. Another two years and you'll be on the shelf. We can't afford to dally any longer."

Mellie had no desire to debate further with her. They

would never see eye to eye on the issue. Now her father had turned against her, as well. She felt as though she were suddenly alone in the world. Biting her lip to keep from crying, she stood and turned to leave.

"Where are you going?" Terry asked. "You haven't finished your breakfast."

"Yes, I have. I have work to do—and very little time to do it." Without giving her sister a chance to respond, she slipped through a side door and ran out to the stables.

Miles felt more impatient unearthing the mosaic than he'd ever before felt about a project. He sat back in the dirt, looking over at Ben's hunched form, several yards away. The maniac hadn't yet taken a break today, and they'd been working practically since dawn. Miles had eaten lunch over an hour ago, while his friend continued slaving over the atrium floor. Today was one of those days he envied Ben for his concentration.

For the hundredth time, his own attention wandered toward the crumbling ancient wall that blocked his view to the east. All morning he'd had an urge to venture around it and check on Melpomene's work, but she couldn't have made much progress since yesterday.

He looked back down at the tiles he'd uncovered and found himself mocked by the lewd smirk of a satyr. His lip curled.

"I'm interested *only* in what she may have found," he muttered to the creature.

"Miles?" Sir William's voice startled him.

He dropped his work gloves on the satyr's face and stood to look up at the man, who stood at the edge of the pit. "Yes, sir?"

"I've been watching you as I approached. You looked as though you were woolgathering."

"I'm afraid I was." A bead of sweat trickled down his brow. He swatted it away. "I suppose I'm having a bit of a bad day."

"How would you like a change of pace—one that would entail doing me a favor?"

"My pleasure. What did you have in mind?"

Sir William climbed down the side of the trench and joined him. "I'd be obliged to you if you could lend Mellie a hand with her project."

"Mellie?" He froze. "Does she need help moving something? Shall I go over to her now?"

"Actually, I was hoping you'd pitch in for the next week or so. You see, Terry's going to give her a London debut, but Mellie's keen to dig up that plate she came across yesterday. Against my better judgment, I've allowed her up to two weeks to finish, with the stipulation that she avoids dallying. Since you've expressed some interest in her project, I thought perhaps you could help to speed her work."

He grappled for words. Two weeks side by side with a woman who paraded about in breeches, pretending to be a scholar but likely only looking for attention. How much serious work would he be able to get done? "Shouldn't ... shouldn't she leave immediately in order to take advantage of the full Season?"

"She should, but she doesn't want to go at all—and I'd like more time with Terry, too. Nevertheless, as soon as Mellie reaches that plate, I'm sending them off. This is just the sort of venture she needs. Your help would mean a lot to me."

The idea agitated him, but Sir William was his host—and, if he agreed, at least he'd be hastening Melpomene's departure. The more work he did, the sooner she'd be gone. What could be a more powerful incentive for him?

He nodded slowly. "Very well. I'll do what I can."

"Excellent. When can I tell her you'll start?"

He glanced over at Ben, who still leaned over the tiles, obviously unmindful of their conversation. Well, there was no use in putting off the inevitable. "I'll head over to her as soon as I clean up here."

"I appreciate it." Sir William shook his hand, then exchanged a few words with Ben before leaving the mosaic.

Miles gathered up his things and slung his equipment pack over his shoulder. Wandering toward the area where his friend worked, he hoped he hadn't made a mistake. He'd seen no way to say no to Sir William, and he did want Melpomene out of the villa . . . but he had to admit he seemed to have a weakness for the chit. He would have to be careful not to let her see it.

In his mind he pictured her as she'd looked when she'd pulled her head out of the cavity the day before, her hair tumbling down about her creamy skin—such a striking contrast to those fascinating aquamarine eyes.

"Beautiful, is she not?" Ben asked, breaking him out of his reverie.

"What?" He stared at his friend. Had they worked together for so long that the man had learned to read his mind?

"Venus here." Ben gestured with his brush toward a huge ceramic face embedded in the ground. "If you're terribly envious of me, I shouldn't begrudge you the pleasure of helping to unveil her. That grotesque satyr of yours is a sorry substitute for the goddess of beauty."

"Oh . . . yes, he's no match for Venus. The fact is I *am* going to take a break from him. I've promised Sir William I'd lend Melpomene a hand."

"Indeed?" Ben sat back and met his gaze. "I thought you could barely stomach her."

He shrugged. "Sir William told me she'll be going away with her sister soon. I'm not such an ingrate that

I can't endure a few days of her presence for her father's sake.''

His friend raised his eyebrows but made no comment. Tugging a watch out of a pocket in his waistcoat, he glanced at the face. "Goodness, half past one already? I'd meant to stop by and take a look at Mellie's project myself this morning.''

"Perhaps you could join me now, and the two of us could move some heavy stones out of her way.''

"First I have a few more things I'd like to do here.'' He put the watch away and leaned back over on his hands and knees. "I'll try to remember to get over there later.''

"Please do, Bennie—for our host's sake. You know how caught up you get in your work.''

His friend grinned at the mosaic. "That's the way of things when there's a lady involved.''

Miles frowned. "I wouldn't know. Tile fails to excite me quite so much as it does you.''

"More's the pity. If it did, you might not be so bilious now.'' Ben glanced up at him again. "Both yesterday and today you've been singularly out of temper.''

"How many tiles can a man cheerfully dust off?''

His friend frowned. "It's unlike you to get overset about nothing, Miles. Is something troubling you?''

"No.'' He turned to leave, bothered by the scrutiny.

"When you see Mellie,'' Ben called after him, "convey my congratulations on finding the plate, won't you? Who knows when I might run into her.''

Scowling, Miles left the pit. Clearly Ben was going to be no help. He'd have to face Melpomene alone.

Almost as soon as he stepped around to the other side of the east wall, he spotted her bonnet bobbing up and down within the trench. When he drew close enough to see her clothing, he felt an absurd tinge of disappointment. Instead of breeches, she wore a plain muslin gown—the most conservative attire he'd ever seen on her.

She heard his footfall and stood to greet him with an unsmiling face. "Hello, Miles."

"Good day. Made much progress yet?"

"None worth reporting. James Groom and I pulled some big rocks out of the pile early this morning, and I've been dragging out smaller ones all day, but, other than the usual shards of pottery and glass, I've come across nothing."

He slid down into the trench. "You don't seem quite as enthusiastic as you did yesterday."

"If so, it's not my work that's dulled my enthusiasm." She bent to the ground and dumped a scoopful of dirt into a sieve. "It's the prospect of being yanked away from the dig."

He squatted down beside her. "Is Lady Moorehead ruffling your feathers again?"

"Ruffling my whole life. She wants me to go into London with her for the Season—*now,* of all times. She plans to parade me about like some man-chasing debutante."

He crossed his arms over his chest. Impressive, how she kept up this anti-marriage theme. Her ruse was almost convincing. "Didn't you tell me your father wouldn't allow such a journey?"

"I never thought he would." She paused to pick a fragment of blue glass out of the dirt and set it in her basket. "I don't know what's come over him lately. He's persuaded that a London Season is the very thing for me. Terry has him believing he's been neglectful in not bringing me out before this."

He tended to agree but knew better than to tell her so. Instead, he said, "He's asked me to help you with your project, in hope that you might reach the plate before you leave.''

"Yes.'' She looked up at him with a grimace. ''What did you tell him?''

"That I'd join you directly.''

Her eyes widened. Blinking, she looked back down and picked at the dirt. ''You're kind to agree.''

"I'm in debt to your father.''

She looked up again and studied his face for a moment. Finally, she gave him a faint smile. ''It's nice to see this side of you.''

"What side?''

"Oh, the loyal side—or whatever. Never mind. I suppose I know you only as a scholar. In any case, I'm very grateful for your help.''

He felt a pang of something—guilt, he supposed. She seemed truly thankful, when his chief motivation was to get her out of his hair. Well, if he could do any good for her in the process, he would. He opened his equipment sack and pulled out a trowel. ''Where shall I start?''

"You could try that area.'' She pointed to a fissure in the rock with dirt pouring out of it.

"Miss?'' a voice from above interrupted them.

Miles looked up and saw her groom.

"What is it, James?'' she asked.

"You still haven't eaten lunch, and Mrs. Burke said to keep reminding you until you did.''

Her shoulders slumped. ''I simply have too much to do. To make things worse, my sister has some urgent errand she needs me for first thing tomorrow morning.''

"Go ahead,'' Miles urged her, eager for the chance to work alone, free of the conflicting feelings she brought upon him. ''I'll clear as much as possible while you're away from the dig. And I'll be out at dawn tomorrow to make up for your being late.''

She raised her eyebrows. "Goodness. You needn't make a Herculean effort. If all this ends up amounting to nothing, I'll feel dreadful."

To avoid meeting her gaze, he stooped down and picked up her sieve. "No need. I'm only doing what pleases me."

She hesitated, then looked up to her groom. "James, go on ahead of me. Tell Burke I'll be there in a minute."

The young man nodded and disappeared beyond the trench.

Melpomene cleared her throat. "I think I owe you an apology, Miles."

He looked up at her, stunned. "Pardon?"

"I should never have questioned your dedication to archaeology yesterday. You've been my only supporter regarding this silver plate theory I have. Your love of discovery is evident. I was simply being churlish. Terry's visit has my nerves frayed, but I shouldn't have taken it out on you."

Another wave of guilt swept over him. He stood and looked her in the eye, perhaps for the first time since he'd arrived at the Park. "No doubt you were simply reacting to my own black mood. I'll accept your apology only if you accept mine."

She smiled and cast her gaze downward, looking uncharacteristically demure. "Let's call it even then, shall we? And we'll endeavor not to repeat our mistakes."

He felt a tug of something else for her—could it be sympathy? He reminded himself that the spoiled chit likely didn't merit any compassion. Still, he'd be best off trying to get along with her for the next week or so.

"Agreed," he murmured.

"Wonderful. I'll see you after lunch." She brushed some dust from her dress and climbed out of the pit.

He watched until she vanished, then he turned back to the dig. The area was a mess. The cave-in had caused one side of the trench to collapse. Likely her original tunnel had been much smaller than the current one. Had she only taken care to brace it properly, she probably would have reached the plate already.

Well, no sense in crying over spilled milk. If he had any say in it, they'd reach their goal within a few days, anyway—but he certainly had his work cut out for him.

Squatting down, he began to dig and sift through dirt.

Six

The next morning Mellie breathed a sigh of relief when she and her sister finally returned to the manor. The "urgent" errand Terry had needed her for had been nothing more than shopping. She'd tried to dodge the excursion, but her father had insisted she needed new clothes for London. Somehow she'd managed to survive the outing without screaming in aggravation. Now each sister carried several bandboxes into the house, and the coachman followed, laden with larger parcels.

"I still say it was cruel of you not to allow me to stop at the milliner's," Terry said, setting down her burdens on a chair in the front hall. "All I wanted was a bit of ribbon to trim one of my older bonnets."

"Naturally." Mellie added her own purchases to the pile. "Much as you needed Mrs. Barnsleigh to work up only one gown for you, yet we wound up at the modiste's for an hour and a half."

"*Merely* an hour and a half, you mean." Terry turned around so the butler could remove her pelisse. "My sole consolation is that Barnsleigh's work is so inferior to that available in town. I shouldn't have gone to her at all, were it not for your desperately needing things to start the Season.''

Mellie took off her own wrap and handed it to a footman, then looked back at her sister. ''I apologize for cutting your shopping time short, but St. Leger is already out at my dig, and I don't want to leave *all* the work to him. I'm very grateful he's agreed to help at all.''

''I'm glad he has, too. With any luck you'll complete your project this week, and you and I can be off to London.''

Anxious to change into digging clothes, Mellie ignored the comment and started up the hall. Before she'd gone two steps, however, a rap at the front door made her pause.

While she and Terry watched, the butler ushered in a man and woman attired in the latest stare of fashion. Tall, blond, and regal in bearing, the female looked vaguely familiar. The man bore a strong resemblance to her—likely a relation.

As Mellie tried to place them, the butler read from their cards, ''Lady Staughton and Viscount Gough.''

''Gwyneth!'' Terry darted into the arms of the woman, whom Mellie now recognized as an old school-mate of her sister's. ''You *did* receive my note. I scarcely dared hope it would find you at the Lodge.''

Mellie closed her eyes in exasperation. Now she would have to at least greet these people, and she remembered Gwyneth as even more meddlesome than Terry. Would she never get out to the field? She would simply have to make her apologies and excuse herself as soon as possible.

Gwyneth returned Terry's embrace with stiff dignity and a peck in the air above her cheek. ''Indeed it did, but not without a great deal of luck. Rodney and I rarely spend any time in the country these days. You do remember my brother Rodney?''

"Yes, of course." Terry turned a glowing face to him, a man Mellie couldn't recall ever meeting. "How do you do, my lord?"

"Very well, Lady Moorehead." The viscount took her hand and bowed over it. Like Gwyneth, he had a well-formed physique, fair hair and bright blue eyes. Both could be called quite handsome, in a haughty way. " 'Tis a great pleasure to have you safely back in England."

"Thank you, my lord." Terry took a step back and put an arm around Mellie's shoulders to draw her forward. "Allow me to introduce you to my younger sister, Melpomene. She makes her come-out this Season."

With an effort not to roll her eyes, Mellie exchanged salutations with him while Gwyneth stepped forward to look her up and down. "Surely this *Incomparable* cannot be that little hoyden who once could never be torn away from her father."

The *Incomparable* had no answer for such an observation, but her sister tittered with pleasure. "Indeed she is, and in some ways she has not changed. But I expect once we get to London, none of that will tell." She smiled and reached out to brush a stray wisp of hair from Mellie's forehead.

Gwyneth's attention remained fixed. "Well, I wish you all the best with your Season, dear. A beauty such as you is sure to be a great success. And, of course, it never hurts to have a large dowry."

Taken aback by the reference to wealth, she shot a glance at her sister, but Terry kept smiling. For her sake, Mellie swallowed her indignation. "Thank you, my lady."

"Oh, you must call me Gwyn, love. Your sister and

I go back such a long way that we're all practically family here.''

"Indeed we are.'' Terry released her sister's shoulders. "And if Lord Gough will agree, I should like to suggest we dispense with all titles among the four of us.''

"A marvelous idea,'' her friend said before the man could reply. "After all, we're all on our way to London, so I imagine we'll be seeing quite a lot of each other. You've no objections, Rodney, do you?''

His lordship acceded with a slight bow. "How could I?''

Terry bent close to Mellie's ear. "Naturally, we must still observe the formalities when in company.''

"Naturally.''

"I'm so pleased to hear you'll be in town with us,'' she said to the others. Walking to the nearest set of double doors and throwing them open, she gestured for her guests to enter the parlor. "Pray, go in ahead of me. I shall have some refreshments brought around.''

Mellie waited while her sister gave brief instructions to the butler, then tapped her on the shoulder. "Terry, I'm afraid I must—''

"Just for a few moments, dear,'' she whispered. "Nothing more than a polite visit . . . please.''

She frowned as Terry turned into the room. *Fifteen minutes at most,* she thought.

When she entered, the others were still moving about, taking in their surroundings. Mellie observed that Lord Gough walked with a slight limp. She recalled hearing that certain town tulips affected one to emulate Lord Byron. At the time she'd doubted anyone could be so ridiculous, but there was no telling how senseless the brother of Gwyneth might be.

"We can only stay a short while,'' the lady in question said. She and her brother settled down on a sofa.

"We're to stop at the Moultons on our way into London. Never fear, however; when we all get to town, Rodney and I shall be with you two constantly."

"The Moultons?" Terry's eyebrows drew together. "Surely you cannot mean the former Margery Arkwright and her husband? Did you not always set them down as the worst of cits?"

"Ah, yes, the very same, and as encroaching as ever. Still, a woman who was schooled in the same girls' seminary as you and I cannot help but pick up *some* polish, so I choose not to cut her out entirely." She threw her hands up as though she couldn't explain her own congenial nature.

A maid entered with silver tea things, and Terry set about pouring. "I must own I am surprised to hear that you bother with her, but I'm hardly in a position to judge who is good *ton* and who is not. Why, having been away four years, I shall scarcely know a soul in London. You cannot imagine how pleased I am to hear you'll be present."

"The feeling is mutual." Gwyn accepted a cup and saucer, giving her brother a look that struck Mellie as pointed. "Rodney and I are rather deprived of good society ourselves. My poor late husband suffered from such ill health that he and I barely budged from our country estate. As a result, I lost touch with most of my old friends."

Taking up her tea, Mellie decided to try to engage the viscount and see if he were indeed as tiresome as his sister. "And you, Lord Gough? Have you, too, been constrained to a provincial life by a retiring spouse?"

Both he and his sister laughed, but Gwyn was the one to answer. "How witty you are, my dear. But no lucky chit has been able to ensnare my brother yet. I say 'lucky,' of course, because I cannot imagine the girl good enough to deserve dear Rodney."

"Really, Gwyn, you are doing it too brown." Lord Gough's tone was grave, but when he turned back to Mellie he smiled. "No, my history has not resembled that of either of these two ladies. Our current situations are similar only because I've been living on the Continent for the past three years. And please do call me Rodney."

She took in his shy grin and began to wonder if he might be cut from a different cloth from the insinuating woman beside him. "Well, Rodney, I envy you. I, too, would like to travel someday. Was it business or pleasure that kept you away from your homeland for so long?"

"With Rodney, 'tis always pleasure." Gwyn gave him a playful nudge with her elbow.

"Untrue." Without so much as a look of acknowledgment for the woman, he shook his head. "My sister defames me. The experience did begin as a Grand Tour, but during the course of my stay I met with an old acquaintance who involved me in a small exporting business. He and I lived in Geneva the majority of the time, capitalizing on a little undertaking here, another there. Nothing remarkable, but enough to cover our living expenses for the most part."

"At the time Rodney didn't have full access to his inheritance," his sister interjected.

He looked downward, apparently more embarrassed by her than by his need to dabble in trade.

"Your adventures sound fascinating," Mellie said, taking pity on him. "I should like to hear all about them sometime when you're at leisure."

"He'll be glad to oblige you there." Gwyn leaned over the tea table, reaching for a Sevres plate adorned with *petits fours*. "Rodney's always happy for an opportunity to boast of his foreign escapades. I entreat you not to get him started now, or we shall never reach the Moultons' in time for dinner.''

''You'll have these ladies thinking I'm a dead bore, Gwyn.'' He looked at Mellie. ''I promise to answer only what you ask me, and that in single sentences.''

Terry took this opportunity to imitate the sibling raillery of her friend. ''Such treatment will only compel Mellie to ask you a score or more questions. She has an excess of curiosity. Not to say she is a bluestocking, but she has a strong interest in many subjects: archaeology, history ... why, just today she tried to talk me into visiting the Tower of London when we get to town. Of course, such a jaunt is not my cup of tea.''

Gwyn touched a napkin to her lips. ''Silly Terry. Why, even I have been to the Tower, and I don't mind telling you I was captivated. Once one has seen the Crown Jewels, no other bauble ever quite shines again. I hope you will still go, Mellie.''

''Without question. I can always take a maid with me.''

The woman pouted. ''What a shame that my schedule is singularly hectic these next few weeks. Otherwise, I'd take you myself. One cannot see the Crown Jewels too often, you know.''

''Thank you,'' Mellie said hastily, ''but you mustn't concern yourself about me. My maid will keep me good company.''

''Still, a servant isn't the same as a *real* companion ...''

Rodney set down his cup and saucer. ''It so happens that my schedule is not nearly as tight as yours, Gwyn. If Mellie will consent, I'll be happy to escort her.''

''Oh, no, my lord. You needn't expend your valuable time indulging me.'' Mellie ignored the kick to her ankle that came from Terry. ''I'm sure a man in your position has many more important things to do with an afternoon—and we actually do have servants whose companionship I enjoy.''

Her ladyship smiled. ''But you wouldn't be so unkind as to claim you enjoy theirs more than my brother's?''

''I certainly would not.'' Mellie had nearly lost all patience with the woman. ''And I'm sure I cannot be suspected of thinking it, since I've never had the pleasure of your brother's escort.''

''All too true,'' Rodney said before his sister could reply. ''That's why you must accept me now. Let me assure you there's nothing I would rather do than escort you to the Tower one afternoon.''

She could make no further objections without appearing ungrateful, and it would have been heartless to wound this poor man who must put up with such a sister. She fixed a smile on her lips. ''I can hardly refuse such a kind offer. We shall set a date as soon as we all reach town.''

Both Terry and her friend radiated with satisfaction.

After several more minutes the visitors rose to leave, and Mellie let her tense body relax. As she accompanied Terry in walking them to the door, she reflected on the one consolation to having an engagement with the viscount: She was very fortunate it wasn't with his sister instead.

Within a half hour of their departure, Mellie had changed into an old gown and arrived at the plate site. As she dismounted from Anima and handed the reins to her groom, she saw Miles poke his head up from within the trench.

Perspiration glistened on his forehead. He pushed back a strand of his thick dark hair, leaving a dark streak of soil on one temple. Nodding to her, he said, "Good morning."

"Good morning." She grabbed her equipment pack and walked to the side of the pit. "My apologies for being so late. I hope you haven't been working too hard."

To her surprise, he smiled. "Let's just say I've had a productive day so far. Allow me to take your satchel for you."

Mellie passed down the bag and descended without aid. She kneeled to view the area around the plate. "Heavens! You've cleared most of the right side of the trench."

"Yes." He squatted and pointed to a new pile of dirt, at least two feet high, above the side of the pit. "The sifted soil is there. I wish I could say I found something of interest, but, again, it's all just shards."

She blinked at the mound in astonishment. The fineness of the grains showed that the earth had been screened thoroughly. "I can hardly credit how much you've achieved in one morning."

"I started at dawn." A wide grin transformed his face so she could hardly discern the sulky man who had arrived at the Park two days before.

She found herself staring into his chocolaty eyes. When he cast off his usual surliness, his good looks grew rather amazing. She forced her attention back to the rubble that still needed excavating. "How did I ever doubt your ambition? At this rate, we'll easily reach the plate before I go. I don't know how to thank you."

"No need, as I've told you before." Taking up a trowel, he stooped and punctured a patch of dirt. "How did your errand go?"

"As well as might be expected." Still astounded by the amount of work he'd turned around, she added one good point to her assessment of the man: diligence. Leaning over her equipment bag, she pulled out an assortment of tools and rags. "All Terry had in mind for me was shopping, if you can believe that. Fortunately, she sets little store in our local seamstress, so I was eventually able to drag her away from the shops. But it was not until we returned home that the worst part of the morning came."

"How so? Don't tell me you thought to wear those fetching breeches of yours again, and your sister coerced you into putting this on instead." He motioned toward her dress.

Her gaze shot to meet his, and the twinkle in his eye startled her. He looked away immediately, however, while she felt her cheeks grow hot. She would almost have believed he was flirting with her—but she knew nothing of such behavior. Likely he only meant to quiz her on the odd clothing she often wore.

Lifting several small stones out of the ground, she tossed them into a wheelbarrow. "No, I regret to say that I chose this sorry castoff myself. What I referred to was an unexpected visit from Terry's old schoolmate and her brother. I was eager to hurry out here to the dig but unable take my leave without appearing rude."

He dropped a scoopful of soil into a sieve and gently shook the contents through. "Are you well acquainted with these visitors of Lady Moorehead's?"

"Better acquainted than I would like."

"A curious comment, if I may say so." He hesitated. "Am I to understand that you don't share your sister's esteem for these people?"

She picked a gnarled coin out of the dirt and immersed it in a nearby bucket of water. "To be fair, I don't know the brother well enough to draw conclusions about him, but Gwyn is how I imagine Terry would be if she had no good traits to redeem her frivolity. Even in the few days you've been here, you may have gained an idea how seldom Terry and I see eye-to-eye.''

Half his mouth tightened in a wry smile. ''An inkling, perhaps.''

Placing the coin in a rag, she rubbed off the remaining dirt. *I seem always to be complaining to him,* she thought, suddenly at a loss for words. She worked quietly for several minutes, wrapping the coin in a fresh cloth and setting it in a basket.

After a moment, he asked, ''Is Lady Moorehead really so different from you?''

''As different as can be. She is more like my eldest sister, although Clio's personality is not so ... so strong. Sometimes I suspect Terry strives a bit too much to distinguish herself. I've heard that sometimes a middle child will yearn for attention.''

''Being an only child, I can offer no view in that area. But if the theory has merit, what does it say of youngest children, such as you?''

She lifted a second coin out of the ground. ''Oh, we babies of the family are fairly showered with attention. If anything, we're quite spoiled.''

''You have no need to try to attract more attention?''

''None at all.'' She paused to look over at him. '' 'Tis probably the same for an only child, I imagine. Your parents must have had plenty of time for you.''

He shrugged. ''They weren't negligent of me, certainly. Do you suppose I am as spoiled as you?''

''I should be insulted by that, I think!'' She smiled but stopped to consider the discussion more seriously. She had always known she'd been coddled, but now that her father had come down hard on her for once, she was feeling the repercussions of being used to indulgence. As for Miles, he undoubtedly could be supercilious. Could it be due in part to his own indulgence as a child? "Perhaps you and I do expect more than we quite merit."

His gaze flew to hers, his eyes wide.

She laughed outright at his reaction. "At least we only sulk rather than push ourselves forward, like some *middle* children I know."

He studied her a moment, as if considering whether to be insulted, astonished, or amused. At last, he lifted an eyebrow and turned back to his work. "Your theory is interesting, if debatable. I'll take it under consideration."

"Just as you've done with my silver plate theory." She smiled to herself, feeling surprisingly in charity with the man. Now that she thought she might understand him better, he didn't seem so foreboding. Besides, he'd done a great deal to help her today. "I couldn't ask for more."

She went back to her work but soon noticed the rapid pace with which he continued to sift through the soil. His diligence impressed her, even made her feel a bit guilty. "You said you've been out here since dawn. Have you taken any breaks?"

"Why?" he asked, continuing to dig. "Are you thinking about having lunch?"

"No, I just got here—but I thought you might like to stop and have yours."

He straightened and wiped his forehead with the back of his hand. His eyes narrowed as he looked at her. "You wouldn't mind my running off as soon as you arrived?"

"Why would I? This is an archaeological dig, not a social occasion."

Again, he raised an eyebrow.

She sat up now, too, surprised at his surprise. "I normally work alone, you know. If anything, having a companion with me will take getting used to. If you want to, you can quit for the day. You've already done more than a full day's work.''

He studied her for a moment longer, almost as though he didn't believe her. Finally he shook his head and pulled off his gloves. ''Well, then, perhaps I'll go back to the gatehouse for lunch. I shall be back in the afternoon, however. We want to reach that plate as soon as possible.''

''Right,'' she said.

As he climbed out of the pit, she glanced at him a last time. What a difference a day could make in a person's viewpoint. Not only had her opinion of St. Leger suddenly changed, her whole situation had seemed to brighten. Yesterday, she'd felt as though it were her against the world. Today, she had a staunch ally.

Who would have thought she'd find that in Lord St. Leger, of all people?

Seven

Two days later Miles watched as Mellie peeled off a glove at the dig site. Long and skintight, the accessory had obviously been designed for dalliance rather than digging. As she took off the mate, her movements appeared achingly sensual. He could imagine her peeling off her stockings in much the same manner. . . .

"Wouldn't work gloves be more appropriate out here?" he asked, annoyed by his straying thoughts.

She tossed the pair on top of her workbasket and looked up at him. "Sometimes they are, but they only come in men's sizes and often prove cumbersome for me. I find these more efficient when tending to details."

"I see." He looked back down at the piece of pottery he'd been uncovering, a find rare enough that it should have engrossed him. Whether he believed Mellie or not, he wasn't sure. Over the course of the last two days she'd done many things to draw his attention to her, always purportedly without intention. He remembered, however, that her sisters had occasionally come out to the field during his previous visit. They'd been known to feign interest in archaeology in order to put themselves in a man's way, and he doubted such antics were beyond Mellie. He suspected she was simply a more subtle temptress than the other Lowery women.

"I can scarcely credit how much progress we've made." She surveyed the area, then looked to him with a smile. "And now you've come across a Minerva-Sulis pot. I never forgave myself for breaking the one you found last time you were here. I hope this one will somewhat make up for that loss."

"You remember that?" he asked, surprised. It was getting harder and harder to reconcile the woman beside him with the unruly child in his fading memory. Though this Melpomene obviously still could be careless, he'd found that at moments she showed considerable expertise, too.

"I had nightmares about the incident for years." She let out a humorless laugh. "Papa kept telling me that every archaeologist damages a valuable artifact at least once in his career, but *my* mishap wasn't easy for me to accept—and I know it wasn't for you."

Remembering his reaction at the time, he felt his first pang of guilt over how he'd treated her. What Sir William had told her was true. Why, as an eager youngster—perhaps around the same age Mellie had been on his last visit—he'd once dropped an icon his father had brought home from Egypt. Miles remembered how humiliated his clumsiness had made him feel. That statue had been rarer than the pot Mellie broke . . . and his father hadn't even scolded him.

"I was too hard on you," he said, frowning. "Sir William is entirely right. Pray forget the incident. I've done worse myself, and this pot will more than make up for that one. What's more, I owe this discovery to you. Had you not drawn me to this spot, I never would have found it."

"That's kind of you to say." Her gaze met his, and

her eyes had a soft look from which he couldn't seem to look away. For an instant, they just stared, then she said, "Our work together has turned out unexpectedly rewarding, hasn't it?"

His breath caught. Was she hinting that they'd found a mutual attraction? Several times every day she'd caught him watching her—enough to glean that she held some allure for him. Their quick progress on the project had put him in such a good mood, too, that once or twice he'd even slipped and said something flirtatious.

He forced himself to tear his gaze away. Encouraging her any further would be dangerous. "Digging at such a rich site can't help but be rewarding."

Silence hung between them for a moment, while he busied himself with the pot.

"Indeed," she said, her voice flatter than before.

This evidence of disappointment made his blood rush, despite himself. Did she actually feel something for him, he wondered, or did she—like most of the women of his class—simply consider him a good catch?

The latter, he thought, vigorously plucking soil from around the artifact. She was Euterpe's sister, after all.

"The noon sun is hot today, isn't it?" she remarked.

Judging the question rhetorical, he didn't bother responding—or even looking up. Carefully, he removed the piece from the ground and picked up a large brush, dusting away finer bits of earth.

When Mellie stood, however, the movement drew his eye. As if continuing her stripping sequence, she pulled off the pelisse she wore. All of her clothing fit her tightly, clearly old garments rescued from the rag-bag for working in the field. As she struggled to pull off the jacket, the top two buttons on her bodice popped open, revealing an expanse of creamy cleavage. The thought of burying his face between her breasts flooded his head.

She didn't notice the mishap—or pretended not to.

"Oh, it's perfect!" she exclaimed, looking at the artifact he'd extracted. She bent down beside him, her torso just inches from him, distracting him even at such a moment.

She's every bit as shameless as Euterpe, he thought. He held the piece out her. "Here, take a closer look."

"Truly, may I?" She accepted the pot, gently placing it in her lap. "What an excellent specimen!"

"The heat is getting to be too much for me, too," he said, completely unable to concentrate. "I shouldn't have left my canteen back with the horses. I'll go and fetch it now."

Her gaze shot to meet his. "Are you unwell?"

"Only hot." He turned to leave.

"Miles?" she called before he could climb out of the trench.

He looked back over his shoulder. "Yes?"

"Thank you." She gave him a smile that lit up her whole face. "It means a lot to me that you didn't even hesitate to entrust this to me."

He had never seen her look so dazzling. She didn't smile all that often, he realized. He swallowed. "Nonsense."

Turning away again, he climbed to ground level. As he crossed the field to where the horses grazed, he tried to pull himself together. He couldn't allow himself to entertain any more sensual thoughts about Melpomene. He'd already slipped and flirted with her once or twice. How long would it be before he physically acted on his desire?

When he reached the horses, he dawdled with them for several moments, regaining his composure. He could only be thankful for the tremendous progress he and Mellie had made on her project. Perhaps they'd reach the plate as soon as the next day, and he would be free of her.

Slowing walking back to the trench with the canteen, he repeated to himself over and over, *One more day—that's all.*

He slid back down into the pit and found Mellie on her hands and knees, rapt in her work. She glanced up at him, and he saw that her bodice remained undone. From this angle he could see clear to her corset—before he averted his gaze.

"I crated the Minerva-Sulis pot to keep it safe." She sat back on her haunches and pointed at a spot next to him. "It's set aside there."

"Thanks."

She looked at him for another moment. "Mind if I have some of that?"

"Oh—sorry. Help yourself." He handed her the canteen.

As she bent back her head and took a swig, her exposed neck drew his gaze. A trickle of perspiration slipped over her collarbone and into her cleavage.

He looked toward heaven, running a nervous hand through his hair. "Set the canteen wherever you like when you're finished. I want to get started on the other side of the shaft."

Moving several feet away, he took up a trowel and began to dig quickly. *One more day*—if he could help it.

Shoveling and sifting, more and more rapidly, he began to widen the hole leading to the plate. After ten minutes or so, his trowel hit upon something hard. He leaned down to look inside and saw it was only a rock. Gently he began digging around it, preparing to loosen it from the side of the opening.

All at once the rock gave way before he expected

and came off in his hand. Without warning the area above it crumpled. He gasped and jumped back, choking on a cloud of dust.

A movement to his left caught his eye. The side of the trench that had survived the first cave-in was collapsing. He reached out as if to stop the landslide, but it was useless. An avalanche of rubble poured into the pit.

When the deluge stopped, dirt stood nearly up to his shins. The shaft was gone entirely, Mellie's plate below twice as much earth as when she had started digging.

He spun around to check if his cohort had been injured.

She stood behind him, out of range of the debris. Her face ashen, she stared at the damage, both hands up to her cheeks. "Oh, my God."

He followed the line of her gaze, and a sick sensation filled him. Only when the rock dropped from his hand did he realize he'd still been clutching it. "How could I be so stupid? All of our work is undone. We were so close to the plate, and now we're back to square one—or worse."

A moment passed, then he heard Mellie's clothing rustle as she moved closer to him. Softly, she said, "It wasn't your fault. This is the second collapse here, and this time we definitely had the shaft well braced. I believe I understand the problem. This area was a dump for the ancients. All of those bits of refuse must make the ground less stable than in the rest of the villa."

Her theory might have been valid, but his blamelessness did nothing to alleviate his anguish. "But we're still further from the plate than ever."

She drew in a long breath. " 'Tis a setback, but I still have a week and a half before I have to leave for London. We can still reach the plate."

A week and a half? He turned and looked at her,

her bodice undone, wisps of hair clinging to her cheeks. Worst of all, she had a wistful look in her eyes that made her appear vulnerable—made him want to pull her into his arms and reassure her.

Yanking his feet out of the rubble, he brushed past her. By no means could he bear another week and a half of this. With no explanation, he climbed out of the trench and strode away toward the horses.

Just as he reached them, Sir William rode up on his own horse and hailed him. "Ho, Miles. Why such haste? Is something awry?"

Miles looked up at the man, too aggravated to disguise his mood. "We've had another cave-in outside the villa, this one twice as bad as the last."

The baronet frowned. "Hell and damnation. How extensive is the damage?"

"All of the progress we'd made has been undone. Now there's more work to do than ever."

His host shook his head. Dismounting, he tied his reins to a nearby post. When he looked up again, he rubbed his chin in thought. "I wonder if I should send Mellie to town immediately."

Miles thought he must have misheard him. "Pardon?"

"Well, who knows what other obstacles might arise before she reaches that plate? Euterpe was just telling me how fortunate we've been that the project has been moving along quickly. She didn't want to say anything before, but, apparently, the most important gatherings of the Season take place in the first weeks. For Mellie's sake, she agreed to delay their start, but the decision has been worrying her."

Miles had never cared about the Season and didn't now, but he saw his chance at rescue and grasped for it. "Good point. It might be best to send Mellie away as soon as possible, rather than have her hopes raised and dashed again. The soil in the area is unstable, I fear. We can't rule out additional collapses.''

Sir William's mouth formed a grim line. "She won't like the idea by half.''

"Perhaps I could continue with the rough work on the project while she's away. Then when she returns she'll have less to do and less time to wait to realize her goal.''

His host nodded. "I'd appreciate that. If those of us closest to her all show her we believe this arrangement is for the best, surely she'll come to accept it. Do you and Ben have dinner plans for this evening?''

"No. Why?''

"Please come up to the main house and eat with us. I'll ask the local vicar and his wife, too. With all of us there to support Mellie, I'll tell her what I've decided. She can express her concerns, and we'll help her see how important it is for her to make her debut directly.''

A wake of uneasiness lapped over Miles. In truth, he considered the idea of a London debut a crock. He thought that parading about the marriage mart cheapened a woman—but he could hardly express such an opinion. He was in Sir William's debt. Not to mention that he wanted Mellie out of his hair. "Thank you, sir. Ben and I will be there.''

"Excellent. I knew I could depend on you.'' The man looked over toward the site of his daughter's dig. "I'd best see how she's faring now.''

Miles watched him walk away, contemplating whether or not he should follow. He, too, wondered how Mellie was handling her misfortune. Even if she used archaeology to gain men's attention, he could see she truly cared about the work. Had she put on a brave face for his sake, then burst into tears after he'd left?

Still staring toward the dig site, he realized she'd

been considerate not to blame the cave-in on him—
more so than *he* had been of her after the first collapse.
He saw now that she may well not have braced the
shaft all that poorly. Likely she wasn't so careless as
he'd believed. He felt a tug of compassion for her.

She has me growing soft on her. The thought unset-
tled him. He turned away and started toward his horse.
She was an intelligent woman, he'd come to see—
much more intelligent than her sister. She might well
have more wile than Euterpe, too.

He untied the reins, figuring dinnertime would be
soon enough to find out how Mellie fared. For now,
he would call it a day. His emotions were running high,
and in such a state he didn't quite trust himself to speak
to her. He doubted he was completely rational. He
knew he wasn't objective.

Why else would he have advised a man to foist a
London Season upon his daughter?

Within the trench, Mellie gathered up Miles' tools,
placing them in his equipment pack. She had a feeling
he wouldn't be coming back that afternoon. He'd been
quite upset about the collapse. His dedication to this
project continued to surprise her, especially knowing
he had doubts about the value of the object they were
seeking.

She spotted the tip of his trowel sticking out from
under the new rubble. Some of his things had likely
been buried in the mishap. As she kneeled down to
pull out the tool, something made her look down at
her chest. Her bodice was half undone!

"Oh, good Lord!" She fumbled to rehook the two
rebellious buttons with haste. They had to have come
undone when she'd jumped back during the collapse.
She could only hope Miles hadn't noticed.

Her cheeks heated at the thought. Several times since they'd been working together, she'd caught him staring at her in such a way that made her swear he was attracted to her. The idea didn't displease her, either— but she knew little about such matters. She could easily be mistaken. Likely, she was.

She picked up his trowel and gazed absently at the blade. Over the past couple of days her views of him had continued changing rapidly. She'd come to enjoy his company, she had to admit. Having another archae- ologist by her side to offer an expert opinion gratified her—and it didn't hurt that he could practically melt her with his smile.

Grimacing over her weakness for him, she used the trowel to search the rubble for other buried tools. The turnaround in her esteem for Miles astonished her. Why, at this rate, she'd soon be reexamining her dis- avowal of marriage. *What a thought!* A husband who dealt in archaeology might actually understand her desire to work in the field.

A twig snapped behind her, and her heartbeat quick- ened. Miles had come back, after all. But when she looked over her shoulder, her father stood at the side of the trench.

"Papa—you startled me."

"I'm sorry, love." He looked around the area, his expression gray. "I mean about the mishap, not just sneaking up on you."

She stood and took a deep breath, looking around once more. "I suppose you can see what happened."

"Yes—well, Miles told me. I met with him by the horse paddock."

Her gaze shot to meet his. "How did he seem?"

"Discouraged, I fear." Sir William slid down into the pit with her. "But the man has his head screwed on tight. He'll likely take the afternoon to grieve a bit, then be out here again first thing tomorrow."

"True enough." She gave a little laugh. "You know, I never imagined he'd be such a hard worker. He's out here at dawn every morning. I thought *I* was an early riser."

Her father smiled at her. "It's good to see you're still able to laugh after such a setback."

She bent back down to continue her work, embarrassed by the reason for her light heart. If she admitted the truth, today's delay didn't bother her in the least. A part of her would hate to see her collaboration with Miles end.

"Can it be that I'm learning patience?" she remarked, hoping her father didn't suspect the truth.

"You're a good daughter, Mellie. I'm proud to see you growing up."

A certain gravity about his tone unnerved her. She looked back up at him. "Is something troubling you, Papa?"

He hesitated. "*Troubling* is too strong a word. *Preoccupying* me, perhaps."

She stood. "What is it?"

He shook his head. "We can talk about it tonight. As a matter of a fact, I'm inviting a few people to the house for dinner—only Miles and Ben and possibly the Dowdens."

"A dinner party—that's unusual for us."

"I want to honor you and Euterpe before you leave for London."

"That's not necessary," she said, though she thought Terry would likely have wished for an even larger party.

He gave her a faint smile—one that looked strangely sad—and turned to climb back out of the trench. "Let's say about eight o'clock."

"Very well." She watched with worry as he hurried away. His behavior was growing stranger every day. Well, perhaps tonight he'd confide whatever it was that concerned him.

As she turned back to her work, the crate holding the Minerva-Sulis pot caught her eye. Why, Miles had been so upset about the collapse he'd even forgotten that. She decided she'd take it back to the gatehouse for him when she left the trench.

When she quit her work for the day she did, in fact, walk the piece all the way there, unwilling to entrust it to the back of a horse. But when she knocked at the gatehouse door, no one answered.

Odd, she thought, surprised he would have gone anywhere else in his state.

She tried once more, then shrugged to herself, turning around toward the main house. She would have to keep the pot for him until that evening—and send a note down here to let him know she had it.

Eight

At quarter to eight that evening, Mellie stood before the mirror in her bedchamber, her maid, Peggy, pinning up her hair. Normally Mellie chose a simple bun, but tonight the young servant had loosened up the style and teased wisps of curls around her face. The elegance of her reflection surprised her. Her gown, fashioned in turquoise satin, had just arrived from the seamstress today.

Terry walked through the open door, and her jaw dropped. "Mellie, you are absolutely magnificent. That gown is perfect for you. How fortunate that our Mrs. Barnsleigh is such a quick-working seamstress."

Mellie gave her a little smile through the mirror. "Perhaps she has one advantage over the London seamstresses, after all."

"Perhaps." Her sister continued gazing at her, a smile fixed on her face.

Mellie turned back toward the mirror. "I feel somewhat foolish in all of this frippery, but I must confess to being more pleased with the effect than I expected. Clothing has never held much interest for me, but I love the neoclassical looks that have come into fashion."

Terry snorted. "Well, thank heaven some other style didn't crop up this year . . . but you have every reason to be pleased. That sea-foam color sets off your eyes to perfection. There's one advantage in being a little older than most debutantes: You won't have to wear white all Season."

The rich color and the cool, smooth feel of the satin *were* rather marvelous.

"I believe I'm actually thankful for that," she said.

While the maid fussed further, Terry took a step away from them. " 'Tis a shame your beauty will be wasted on only us, the Dowdens and Father's archaeological cronies tonight. I've come to understand why you laughed before when I mentioned Lord St. Leger's eligibility. He and Mr. Romney are pleasant enough, but all they ever talk about is digging things up. The *on-dit* in the village is that the earl is a confirmed bachelor. Judging by his bookish nature, I shouldn't doubt it."

Mellie peeked at her through her lashes, tempted to ask for the details of what she'd heard. But the last thing she wanted was for Terry to glean that she might have an interest in Miles. She chose not to reply.

Her sister began to pace the floor. "You'd think Father could have pulled together a few more guests for my first dinner party back in England. I know he doesn't care for Mr. and Mrs. Whitlam, and the Ainsworths have moved out of Dorset . . . but there must be *some* good society left in this neighborhood. Why are the Shenstones not coming?"

"The daughters are all married off, and Lord and Lady Shenstone died of a fever years ago. The estate was entailed to a pompous nephew whose society we do not pursue."

"Good heavens. One leaves a neighborhood for a

few years and everything changes. When did this tragedy strike?''

"I believe it was some *six* years ago, Terry—before you left." Through the mirror, she grinned at her sister. "Right around the time you made your come-out."

"Oh." She shrugged. "Well, naturally, I was preoccupied that year—and, to be truthful, during most of the time Moorehead courted me. Looking back, I daresay it would have behooved me to keep more in touch with my neighbors and old friends."

"With whom *have* you kept in touch?" Mellie asked as the maid laid a sapphire necklace across her throat. "I know *we* would have liked to hear from you more often."

"I used to write to Aunt Pelham fairly regularly before she died. Over the years, I lost track of most of my friends, except Gwyneth. Thank goodness she and I corresponded, or you and I would be going to London with *no* idea what to expect."

Mellie wriggled while Peggy struggled with the necklace catch. "Until the other day, I hadn't heard about her husband's death, though I knew he was considerably older than she."

"Oh, yes, Lord Staughton died last winter." She raised her eyebrows in a minor show of triumph. "Now *there,* finally, is something *I* knew and *you* did not."

"Quite true." Released from Peggy's ministrations at last, Mellie turned to face her sister. "Now that I stop to think, I'm not surprised the poor man should meet his Maker quickly with such a wife as Gwyn."

Terry scowled. "Oh, Mellie, what an uncharitable sentiment. I don't know why your opinion of Gwyneth leaves so much to be desired. She has never done anything to hurt you."

"I don't claim she has. To say she does nothing *for* me would be more accurate."

Her sister opened her mouth as though to protest again but appeared to change her mind and simply sighed. "In any case, I'm glad you accepted Rodney's invitation to see the Tower of London. He is a handsome devil, is he not?"

"Handsome enough. Take care not to raise your hopes, however. He'd have to be well nigh perfect for me to consider taking on such a sister-in-law."

Terry waved off the comment. "Enough of this nonsense. We ought to be getting to our guests, such as they are."

"Yes, ma'am." Mellie turned to the maid and smiled. "Thank you, Peggy. I won't need anything else."

The girl gave her a shy grin. "You do look wonderful, miss." She bobbed a curtsy and backed out of the room.

Terry immediately stepped toward the door, too. "Well, let us go show you off to Papa, the Dowdens, and your archaeological mates. Lord, what an assembly."

Mellie followed slowly, feeling shy yet also eager to see what reactions her appearance drew. She could hear the sound of laughter below and picked out Miles' voice among the others, though she couldn't make out any of his words.

When they entered the parlor, the rest of the party was already there, the men sipping brandy and Mrs. Dowden ratafia. Everyone commented on everyone else's elegance, but Miles' gaze lingered on her longer than on anyone else, sending a tingle up her spine. As for him, he looked dashing in formal evening wear. The well-tailored black attire provided a flawless complement to his dark good looks.

Once they had all exchanged greetings, the party moved into the dining room.

Mellie found herself seated next to Miles and couldn't help but be pleased. It seemed strange to be so focused on this man, but right now she had more in common with him than with anyone else present. She wondered if he might make one of his teasing comments to her tonight. If her sister witnessed it, maybe Terry could tell her whether or not he truly was flirting.

As one footman served the first course—a pumpkin soup—another poured champagne all around the table. When all had glasses, Sir William lifted his. "To my lovely daughters—and to the realization of two long-awaited events: the safe arrival home of the one and the formal presentation of the other."

Murmurs of accord resounded, amidst the clink of full-lead crystal.

Mellie sipped her drink, trying to smile but failing. The mention of her London debut stirred up an uneasy feeling in her stomach. For days she'd succeeded in banishing the idea from her head, but as the time of her departure neared, ignoring it grew more difficult. She didn't want to make a social debut. This little gathering at her father's house represented about the most attention she ever wanted converging on her.

The weight of Miles' gaze drew her notice to him. He wasn't smiling either, she noted. Was that sympathy she read in his eyes? What else could it be?

He turned to the others. "I'd like to propose the second toast: To Mellie's find. May she unearth the richest discovery of the year in Romano-British archaeology."

The unexpected wish drew a laugh from her. How thoughtful of him to take note of the matter that meant most to *her*. Smiling at him, she nodded and drank again. "May *we,* you mean."

"Mais oui, mademoiselle." Golden glints sparkled in his chocolate eyes.

She couldn't seem to look away while another round of clinks and murmured comments sounded around them.

He touched his glass to hers and said in a low voice, "You look stunning, Mellie."

Her cheeks heated. Looking down, she took a gulp of champagne. She didn't favor the bubbly stuff above half, but she knew alcohol was supposed to lend one fortitude and merriment. At this point in her life, she could use some of both.

"Thank you," she whispered.

"Lady Moorehead, you've weathered your voyage remarkably well," the parson's wife said from across the table. She was a plump woman with an amiable face and medium brown ringlets frosted with a tinge of gray. "One would never know you've been traveling. You are the picture of health."

"How kind of you to say, Mrs. Dowden." Dimples puckered Terry's cheeks. "I enjoyed a relatively calm crossing, and I always have been a staunch traveler."

"Not much affected by *mal de mer?*" Mr. Dowden's countenance matched his wife's for cheerfulness, though crinkling lines revealed him to be more advanced in years.

"Not at all. Between the two crossings I made, I had not a sick day."

Mrs. Dowden shook her head. "I wish I had your constitution. Mr. Dowden and I went to Holland for our wedding journey, and I had a terrible time going over the North Sea."

"The crew told us it was one of the roughest days they had witnessed in years." Mr. Dowden gave Terry a wink. "But why don't we speak of something more pleasant? Pray tell us something about your life abroad, my lady.''

While they ate, Terry related her impressions of the West Indies, characteristically focusing more on the society than on the land itself. After she had fielded a number of questions, the parson turned to his wife. ''The Lowery girls are glowing tonight, are they not, my dear? Not only is Lady Moorehead looking her finest, Miss Melpomene is lovely.''

''Oh, yes. I've noted how Miss Lowery has come into bloom. That is a vastly becoming gown, dear.''

''Thank you, ma'am.'' Embarrassed, Mellie studied her champagne. ''My sister has been helping me modify my wardrobe to suit the tastes and requirements of London.''

''She has done a wonderful job.''

Terry smiled. ''The task has been easy. With the face and form Mellie has, 'tis not hard to make her shine.''

Indeed, Mellie spent the next few minutes shining red while her father, her sister, and the Dowdens reflected on the finer points of her person. She didn't dare look toward Miles, though she sensed his gaze on her. Diverting her attention to her champagne again, she found her glass empty.

Almost instantly, a footman stepped up to refill it. She smiled at him and returned to sipping. If this tickly beverage could restore some of her composure, then she would gladly drink it.

''How are your Roman ruins coming along, Sir William?'' Mr. Dowden asked, earning her gratitude for the change of subject. ''I've heard no news of them in some time.''

The baronet sat back to allow the serving of another course. ''Very well, indeed. This year is likely to bring some of our most impressive finds yet. Ben is uncovering a beautifully preserved mosaic floor, and Mellie recently located some metal plating that promises to be of great interest when extracted from the ground.''

"So you are still following in your father's footsteps, Miss Lowery?'' Mrs. Dowden asked her. "Your explorations must be fascinating. Can you tell us more about the ruins?''

"My pleasure.'' For the first time all evening, she smiled without accompanying butterflies in her stomach. "Basically, the Park encompasses a fairly typical Roman villa—an ancient manor house, if you will. Very little of the building remains, but near the middle of the site one wall still stands. Centering around that point, we've found much pottery and glass—most of it badly broken—plus additional crumbled walls, the mosaic my father mentioned, and the hypocaust of a bathhouse.''

"What is a hypo—a hypocaust?'' the woman asked.

Sir William sipped his champagne and smiled at her. "An ancient Roman heating system. Quite amazing, really. It consists of several furnaces that heat a special space left open beneath a building. The heat circulates throughout the area, evenly and effectively warming the rooms through the flooring.''

"Wondrous.'' Mr. Dowden raised his glass and nodded.

"What I wouldn't give for such a system when I have to get out of bed on a cold morning.'' Terry held out her glass for the footman to refill. "I dread setting my bare feet down on icy floorboards.''

Ben shook his head. "Hypocausts were generally used only in bathhouses. The system was too elaborate to rig throughout the villa.''

"Oh.'' With a look of disappointment, she stared into her champagne. "What a pity.''

Sir William cut into the steak on his plate. "Why

don't you tell the Dowdens about the mosaic, Ben? 'Tis by far the most exquisite work yet uncovered here.''

"Gladly, sir." He went on to describe the masterpiece of tile in detail. The Dowdens posed more questions, and before the end of dinner the discussion about the villa grew quite lively.

The indulgence in Mellie's favorite topic combined with the champagne to remedy her lack of ease. She still sensed Miles watching her often but felt gratified rather than intimidated. As the general conversation grew more lively, he frequently leaned over to her with a confidential comment, and she laughed with him comfortably.

"Bennie has enthralled everyone tonight," he said at one point. "Even your sister appears genuinely interested in ancient Roman technology."

She giggled, enjoying the light dizziness that had come over her. "I believe she's hoping her husband will take a lesson from them and build a hypocaust under her chambers. Did you see her eyes light up when you described Roman plumbing?"

"Poor Moorehead. He'll have a devil of a time finding an engineer capable of concocting a running water system for him."

Their shared amusement was interrupted when Terry stood and proposed that the women withdraw.

As everyone rose, Sir William looked around the table. "If no one objects, I suggest we men take our port with the ladies tonight. I have a matter I'd like to discuss with everyone."

The gravity of his tone tempered Mellie's merriment. "Is something wrong, Papa?"

"Not at all, love. Everything is for the best."

His evasive response didn't comfort her, but when she glanced at Miles she forgot it. He had a hand up to his brow and his gaze cast downward. "Miles, are you quite all right?"

He looked up at her—and to a circle of concerned faces. "Only warm. I ought to have worn a lighter jacket."

"Let us go outside for a breath of air." Besides being concerned for him, she wanted a moment by herself before her father discussed whatever preoccupied him. Despite his reassurances, she had a foreboding feeling about the matter.

"That isn't nece—" Miles started.

"No, go on," Sir William interrupted him. "Join us in the parlor when you've recovered."

"I'm quite fine, sir, truly."

"Well, *I*, too, am warm." Mellie tucked her arm through his. "Perhaps you'll indulge me with a turn about the terrace?"

He hesitated again but nodded and let her lead him out of the room.

As they walked through the house, she thought he held himself rather stiffly; likely the attention he'd drawn had made him feel awkward. For her part, she savored the warmth of his arm against hers. Normally she might have felt shy about holding on to him so closely, but the pleasant dizziness from the champagne had indeed brought courage with it.

They stepped out onto the terrace, neither of them speaking. A cool breeze fanned her face, and the sound of crickets filled the air. The sky was clear but moonless, and the darkness made her feel very isolated from all but her companion.

After a moment of breathing in the fresh night air, she asked, "Are you certain you're not ill?"

"Quite." He met her gaze, a small crease forming between his eyebrows. "We should go back inside."

"We've only just come out." She studied him more

closely. "Are you, too, worried about what my father's going to say?"

He looked out at the shadowy gardens. "He said there was no cause for concern."

Another evasive answer. She followed his example and gazed out at the darkness. "I have a bad feeling about this."

"It's useless to speculate." Pulling his arm free from hers, he stepped up to the stone half wall that stood at the edge of the terrace. "Unless you want to go in and hear him now, we might as well speak of something else."

He sounded irritated, though she didn't understand why. She considered going back inside but still didn't feel ready. "Very well. Why don't we talk about London? You have a house in town, and I imagine you've spent considerable time there. Perhaps you can suggest some more scholarly pursuits for me than those my sister has in mind."

Taking a deep breath, he turned to face her and leaned back against the wall. "Of course. The city has countless cultural advantages. There are museums and private collections to view, good lending libraries to borrow from, plus the opera and plays to attend. I know you're not keen to go into town, but I daresay you'll enjoy your visit."

"Do you think so?" She looked up at him, trying to smile. When her gaze met his, however, a pang of wistfulness pierced her. Not only did she not want to leave her project, she didn't want to leave *him*. What if he decided to end his time here before she returned? In truth, she didn't want to miss *any* of his stay. "I still don't want to go."

His mouth tightened into a grim line, and he broke their shared stare, looking downward. "Our desires don't always match what we must do."

She wished he would have told her that he didn't want her to go, either—but he hadn't, so she gulped down that desire. Moving next to him at the wall, she asked, "What do you recommend I do in town?"

"Well . . . there are Lord Elgin's Marbles, of course. Have you seen them before?"

"No. My father has visited them more than once, but my sisters always insisted the nudes were inappropriate for me to view." She let out a snort. "They don't seem to realize how many Roman friezes I've seen."

"Er . . . of course. In any case, the Marbles are glorious. I'm sure you know what to expect from the Parthenon. Then there's the Egyptian Hall in Piccadilly and—oh, I just remembered . . . the Belzoni exhibition comes to London this month."

"So it does!" Mellie's gaze shot to meet his, her eyes wide. "I read about it several weeks ago, but since I had no thought of going into town at the time, it slipped my mind. I understand Mr. Belzoni has constructed a model of an Egyptian burial chamber, complete with a genuine sarcophagus."

He nodded, rubbing his chin. "It almost makes me wish *I* were going to London."

"Why don't you?" she asked, excited by the thought. "We could attend the exhibition together."

He looked at her for a moment, then shook his head. "You tempt me, but I cannot."

"Why ever not?"

Sighing, he turned back toward the darkness. "I have my work here."

Disappointment washed over her, but she couldn't very well argue with the same excuse she'd given her family when they suggested she leave the Park. "Well, now you know how I feel—except *you* get to do as you please."

"You think so?" He peered at her out of the corners of his eyes.

"You get to stay here and dig, don't you—while I'm forced to go to town?"

"Perhaps I truly want to go to the exhibition, but I think my work here is too important to abandon."

He's quizzing me again, she thought. She grinned at him. "Are you trying to tell me that *his lordship, the only child,* doesn't always do exactly as he pleases?"

His gaze flit over her face. "Never, lately, it seems."

The intensity in his eyes made her draw in her breath. "What have you been wanting to do?"

He studied her for a moment longer, and despite her inexperience, she knew he wanted what she did. His gaze skimmed her lips, and somehow she knew he would kiss her.

"Only this." Stepping toward her, he bent down and met her mouth with his.

She couldn't quite believe it was happening, but she responded, leaning into him. His lips were softer than she'd imagined and tasted faintly of champagne. He smelled of shaving soap and felt warm, so warm, when she laid her hands lightly on his chest. She could feel hard muscle through his shirt. How different from her own soft flesh—how *wonderful* . . .

Her mind reeled as he deepened the kiss, parting her lips with his tongue. *Goodness,* she thought, *he feels about me as I do about him.* Elation like she'd never known coursed through her body. . . .

Then he pulled away—gently, but most definitely, away.

He took a deep breath and dropped his hands from her waist. Turning back to the wall, he shook his head. "It seems you were right about my personality, Melpomene. I'm a spoiled, weak-willed brat. Despicable."

At that moment the door to the house opened, and

Terry popped her head outside. "Ah, there you two are. I'm glad to see you're well, my lord. Come back inside, won't you? The Dowdens have to leave shortly, and Father wants them here for our discussion."

She stood at the door waiting, so they had no choice but to move toward her.

As they stepped inside, Miles said quietly, "Forgive me."

Her whole being felt pulled down by a weight. She knew little about the interactions between the sexes, but clearly something had gone wrong just now.

She searched his eyes, trying to understand, but he turned away again, motioning for her to precede him through the door.

Mechanically, she followed her sister up the hallway. Why didn't Miles feel the euphoria she had felt? Had she made some grave error out on the terrace? She knew nothing of kissing. Why had she ever thought she'd know how to respond to him? She should have explained how naive she was, how unlike other young females, who spent hours tittering and gossiping about boys. By rejecting their chatter had she missed out on some mysterious knowledge about men and women?

"Ah, there you are." Her father rose from his armchair as they entered the parlor. "Are you both revitalized now?"

Mellie gave him a wavering smile but didn't speak—nor did Miles.

"Come and have a seat, love." Terry placed a hand on her shoulder and steered her toward a long couch.

Her mind racing in several directions at once, Mellie allowed herself to be led. She perched on the edge of the couch, and her sister settled beside her.

Focusing on Miles, across the room, she watched him accept a brandy snifter from her father. She took advantage of the distance between them and eyed his noble profile. He raised the snifter to his mouth, and she thought, still in awe, *I have tasted those lips. . . .*

A painful yearning welled up inside her. *I had him and lost him in an instant.*

"Mellie, I mean particularly to appeal to you now." Her father's voice broke into her thoughts. He returned to the chair he had vacated. "Those of us present are the people most concerned for your well being—less Clio, naturally. We are here to convince you how important your debut in London is."

She frowned, confused as to his point—but her brain was a muddle. "Forgive me, but that seems a curious premise for a gathering."

The baronet cleared his throat. "You may want all of our support when I tell you what I decided today. When I heard of the second cave-in at your dig, the setback distressed me very much. I had already come to doubt my wisdom in delaying your debut, but the project seemed to be swimming along . . . until now. This second mishap has shown me that this event is too important for us to rely on good luck. I've spoken to several people, and we all agree that the *possibility* of reaching your plate in the next week isn't worth the risk of missing out on important social advantages."

He looked around at the others. "Isn't that so?"

Mellie had a vague perception of their nodding and murmuring approval. She got to her feet, shaking off the arm Terry proffered. "What does this mean? Are you moving up the date of my departure?"

He nodded, his gaze squarely centered on her. "You and Terry will leave first thing tomorrow morning."

She gaped at him, aware of the others staring at her in turn. She felt like a cornered animal. The people closest to her had ganged up on her! Glancing around the room, she saw that Miles was the only one who wasn't watching her, his gaze fixed on the floor.

"Your father's decision is for the best, my dear," Mrs. Dowden said gently. "Your ruins will be waiting here when you return in six weeks. I know that the days pass more slowly for the young, but 'tis a very short time, truly."

Mellie looked at her, then around at the others. "And you all think so? Miles, do *you* agree with my father?"

His gaze shot to meet hers, his eyes wide, almost helpless in appearance. He glanced at her father, then looked back at her. "Given all that has happened today, I believe this is for the best."

The words he'd chosen didn't escape her: *all that has happened.* He had made it clear he considered their kiss a mistake. Heat suffused her face. She felt powerless, mortified. He didn't feel at all the way she did. She had made a complete fool of herself over him . . . and she had no ally regarding her work, after all.

She took a deep and ragged breath. She was defeated, but she wouldn't let them see it. Lifting her chin, she faced her father. "Well, then, it seems I have packing to do. I'm sure you will all excuse me."

"Mellie, wait, don't walk away—" her sister said, but Mellie had already left the room.

In the hall, she could no longer maintain her composure. She ran up the stairs and into her bedchamber, locking the door behind her. Diving onto the bed, she pulled two fluffy down pillows over her head. The tightening in her throat gave way, and she sobbed into the mattress, tears streaming.

She would be all alone now . . . and away from home, without even her work to comfort her.

Nine

Lying on his side in bed, Miles watched the first traces of daylight stretch across the wall in front of him. Rather than sleeping, he'd passed the night ruing the events of the previous day. First he had kissed a well-bred female, breaking his own paramount rule of behavior. Then, the look in Mellie's eyes upon hearing her father's decree had filled him with guilt. Her obvious despair made him realize her work meant the world to her, and that encouraging her father to banish her from her project had been abominably selfish.

He rolled over onto his back and stared up at the ceiling. His worries about controlling his weakness for her may have proved valid, but if anyone were forced to leave Lowery Park it should have been *him*. After Mellie had fled the room, he'd pulled Sir William aside and asked him to rethink his decision. Unfortunately, the man had made up his mind.

His thoughts strayed back to the kiss for the thousandth time. The vivid memory of Mellie's mouth on his, her breasts crushed against him, the fresh scent of her hair—all of the details of contact with her filled

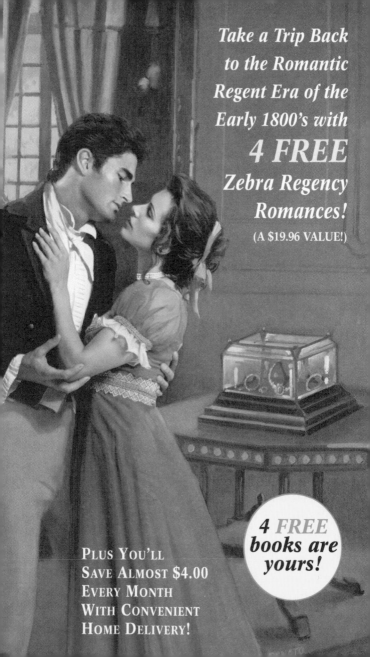

Take a Trip Back to the Romantic Regent Era of the Early 1800's with

4 FREE

Zebra Regency Romances!

(A $19.96 VALUE!)

4 FREE books are yours!

PLUS YOU'LL SAVE ALMOST $4.00 EVERY MONTH WITH CONVENIENT HOME DELIVERY!

We'd Like to Invite You to Subscribe to Zebra's Regency Romance Book Club and Give You a Gift of 4 Free Books as Your Introduction! (Worth $19.96!)

If you're a Regency lover, imagine the joy of getting 4 FREE Zebra Regency Romances and then the chance to have these lovely stories delivered to your home each month at the lowest price available! Well, that's our offer to you and here's how you benefit by becoming a Regency Romance subscriber:

- **4 FREE** Introductory Regency Romances are delivered to your doorstep (you only pay for shipping and handling)

- 4 BRAND NEW Regencies are then delivered each month (usually before they're available in bookstores)

- Subscribers save almost $4.00 every month

- You also receive a **FREE** monthly newsletter, which features author profiles, discounts, subscriber benefits, book previews and more

- No risks or obligations...in other words, you can cancel whenever you wish with no questions asked

Join the thousands of readers who enjoy the savings and convenience offered to Regency Romance subscribers. After your initial introductory shipment, you receive 4 brand-new Zebra Regency Romances each month to examine for 10 days. Then, if you decide to keep the books, you'll pay the preferred subscriber's price, plus shipping and handling.

It's a no-lose proposition, so return the FREE BOOK CERTIFICATE today!

Say Yes to 4 Free Books!

Complete and return the order card to receive this
$19.96 value, ABSOLUTELY FREE!

If the certificate is missing below, write to:
Regency Romance Book Club
P.O. Box 5214, Clifton, New Jersey 07015-5214
or call TOLL-FREE 1-800-770-1963
Visit our website at www.kensingtonbooks.com.

FREE BOOK CERTIFICATE

YES! Please rush me 4 Zebra Regency Romances (I only pay for shipping and handling). I understand that each month thereafter I will be able to preview 4 brand-new Regency Romances FREE for 10 days. Then, if I should decide to keep them, I will pay the money-saving preferred subscriber's price for all 4...that's a savings of 20% off the publisher's price. I may return any shipment within 10 days and owe nothing, and I may cancel this subscription at any time. My 4 FREE books will be mine to keep in any case.

Name _____

Address _____ Apt. _____

City _____ State _____ Zip _____

Telephone ( ) _____

Signature _____
(If under 18, parent or guardian must sign.)   RN122A

Terms and prices subject to change. Orders subject to acceptance by Regency Romance Book Club.
Offer valid in U.S. only.

Treat yourself to 4 FREE Regency Romances!

A $19.96 VALUE... FREE!

No obligation to buy anything, ever!

lll..l..lll...ll.l.l.l.l..l.l.l..ll.l..l.l..ll.l.ll..l

REGENCY ROMANCE BOOK CLUB
Zebra Home Subscription Service, Inc.
P.O. Box 5214
Clifton NJ 07015-5214

PLACE
STAMP
HERE

him with desire like he'd never felt before. Was it the forbidden aspect of her—the danger of falling into her trap—that made him want her so much? On the one hand, he felt appalled that he had compromised her so; on the other, he blamed her for tantalizing him over the past week. Had she possibly even set him up for this? Had an offer of marriage been what she'd sought last night?

He shook his head to himself. Though he still doubted her declarations against marriage, if she'd wanted to ensnare him she would have kicked up such a fuss the whole party would have known about his transgression. Instead she'd returned to the others and weathered blow after blow from a mob rallied against her. Then she had quietly walked away holding her head high.

Her integrity shamed him. He'd acted in a despicable way—and he hadn't even properly apologized. Many people would have said he owed her an *offer of marriage* now. The least he owed was a proper apology. He had to see her this morning before she left for London. What exactly he would say he didn't know— though he wasn't going to offer for her, of course. After years of swearing off marriage, a reversal at a moment's notice would undoubtedly be a mistake. And if Mellie's rails against the institution proved sincere, she might even scoff at the gesture.

He sat up and swung his legs over the side of the bed. Catching his own eye in a mirror across the room, he saw his disheveled reflection and grimaced.

With my looking this way, she would never accept me anyway.

Still unsure how he would approach her, he got out of bed and threw on his clothes. He went downstairs and stepped out the back door into the garden of the gatehouse.

The dew-bedecked foliage and chirping birds cast a

spell of tranquility over the scene, but as he sat down on a cold, damp bench, he could think of no magic solution to his problems. The only sure way to clear up this coil would be to march up to the manor and beg Sir William's permission to pay addresses to his daughter.

"Ho, there!"

A cheerful voice coming from the back door prompted him to look up as Ben emerged from the gatehouse. On one slim shoulder, he balanced an unwieldy crate overflowing with brushes, trowels, picks, and rags.

"Good morning, Miles." He tottered over to the bench and dropped his burden on the ground.

"Morning."

Sitting down, Ben looked into the box of equipment. "I got up early to take inventory before I go into the village for supplies. I must say I didn't expect to find you awake."

"I couldn't sleep."

He glanced up from his gear. "You look as though you've been up all night. Why the devil aren't you in bed?"

Miles drew in a deep breath and released it slowly. "Frankly, I have half a mind to try to catch up with Mellie before she leaves. You will scarcely believe my stupidity, but I . . . er, was not quite the gentleman with her last night. I've no idea how to apologize."

Ben began rummaging through the equipment, oddly showing no sign of shock. "Considering your state of mind lately, I'm surprised it didn't happen sooner— but I'll wager you're making too much of the incident. Mellie's not likely to hold one little lapse in manners against you."

"A *'lapse in manners'*? Perhaps I've not made it quite clear what happened."

His friend shrugged his shoulders, now separating his supplies into several piles on the ground. "I think I can surmise. You and Mellie had a row over how to proceed with her project, right? The fact is that she's a seasoned professional. She is well aware that differences of opinion arise in the field. There's every reason to believe that she'll make allowances for you."

Miles leaned back on the bench, running a hand through his hair. "No, Ben, I fear the circumstances aren't quite so simple. It's more my *behavior* that was at fault."

"I see." He folded a rag and set it atop a stack of others. "You *have* been a right curmudgeon lately. I daresay that if you behaved as disagreeably with Mellie last night as with me last week, then you do owe her an apology."

"Oh, I behaved badly—though hardly in the same manner I did with you." Miles rubbed his temples. "In this case, I was far worse."

"Really?" Ben looked at him. "Well, you're in no state to see the ladies before they set off. You might send a note over with me. I mean to see if Mrs. Burke needs anything from the village before I go."

"No, a note won't suffice."

"Then perhaps a bouquet." Ben finished organizing and started placing his gear back in the box. "Flowers often mollify a vexed woman, and there's a fine selection growing here. All you need do is gather up the finest ones and add your note. I shall be pleased to act as courier."

Miles eyed the colorful blossoms surrounding them. "I suppose the idea is worth a try, but I'd best deliver the arrangement myself. I want to make sure she knows I'm sincere. Would you mind waiting for me?"

"Not at all." Ben boosted the crate back up on his

shoulder and started back toward the gatehouse. "I should think you'd be in a bigger hurry than I."

"Indeed." With a glance up at the brightening blue sky, Miles sprang to his feet. He lost no time gathering up the boldest of the garden's offerings—as if even the most impressive bouquet could stand up to this office.

As the sun rose, Mellie sat wilting at the foot of her bed. She knew she should be dressed and downstairs but felt far too sick to move. Sick at heart mostly, though she did have a substantial headache as well.

She'd managed to sleep fitfully and had had several unsettling dreams about kissing Miles. This morning she wanted him more than ever—but she knew she had no hope. During the wakeful intervals of the night, she had replayed dozens of scenes from the past week in her mind, hoping to recall some hint that he might be truly interested in her. But as far as she could see, his behavior had been strictly professional. He'd never asked her to go riding with him or given her a gift—none of the sorts of things men did when courting a woman.

Clearly, he had kissed her solely on some sort of whim. Who knew why males did what they did? Certainly not she—and she'd be better off not wasting her time in speculation. Setting her jaw, she told herself she had loftier goals than trying to read male behavior—a preoccupation more suited to her sisters.

A sharp rap sounded on the bedroom door, and the knob turned before she could respond. Terry opened the door, took one look at her, and stopped on the threshold. "Why are you not dressed?"

Mellie put a limp hand up to her loose hair and looked down at her chemise without answering.

Terry strode up to face her, crossing her arms over her chest. "I don't suppose you've forgotten the plans we made last night to depart by half-past six?"

Wincing, Mellie pressed her fingers into her brow. "Must you be so loud? I can hear you perfectly well when you speak in a normal tone."

"Perhaps I'd find that easier if I had a sister who behaved normally." She surveyed the room until she spotted Mellie's valises behind the door. "At least your bags are packed, thanks to Peggy, no doubt. I presume you've not had breakfast. You know that I don't intend to stop for lunch until late this afternoon."

"I won't require breakfast—and perhaps not lunch, either." She forced down an unpleasant lump in her throat. "To be honest, I don't believe I could eat a bite."

Terry frowned and leaned closer to scrutinize her eyes. "Oh, no. Don't tell me you had too much to drink last night."

"Perhaps a wee bit too much."

Her sister shook her head. She hesitated, then took a step away. "I suppose I need not waste my time lecturing you on the evils of drink. Traveling in such a condition, you're likely to feel them well enough for yourself today. I only hope this experience serves as a lesson to you."

Mellie nodded.

Terry turned to exit the room. "I still expect you to be ready in no longer than ten minutes. Meanwhile, I shall have Mrs. Burke pack us a cold collation in hope that you regain your appetite quickly. Traveling is hard enough on the constitution without adding poor eating habits to boot."

"Thank you."

She paused in front of the door. "The only saving grace is that this happened here at home. Do you realize what a fool you might have made of yourself had you pulled such a stunt in London?''

Without waiting for an answer, she stalked out of the room, letting the door slam behind her.

Mellie jumped, then stared at the wooden panels with a sigh. "Yes, Terry. I believe I have a good idea."

She stumbled out of bed and splashed her face with cool water. Soon Peggy brought her a cup of tea and helped her pull on her travel clothes. By the time they'd finished her toilette, she felt a little more like herself.

Making her way downstairs on unsteady legs, she stepped out the front door at last. Terry was nowhere in sight, and she breathed a sigh of relief, hoping she had avoided further recrimination.

Her father stood beside the carriage, supervising the loading of luggage. When she spotted him, fresh pain stabbed through her. Under normal circumstances, she would have wept at the thought of leaving him, but his new coldness toward her hurt her in a different way—one that left her numb and dry-eyed.

He looked up and noticed her. "Good morning, Mellie."

"Good morning, sir."

A frowned creased his brow. He looked down, then met her gaze again. "I shall miss you girls until I come and join you—perhaps in a fortnight or so."

She resisted running into his arms as she might have done before yesterday. "I'm sure we'll look forward to your visit."

The smile he gave her didn't reach his eyes. "London will keep you so busy you'll have few thoughts to spare for your old father."

Her mouth tightened. "I don't forget my family as readily as some people seem to."

He drew in a deep breath. "Well, since we'll be together again soon, there's no sense making a fuss over our parting now. Perhaps I should help you into the carriage?''

She let him hand her inside, though his light touch on her elbow seemed to burn more than comfort her. When he turned away to instruct the coachman, she sank back against the squabs, trembling with checked emotion.

''Mellie!'' a masculine shout sounded in the distance.

She froze. The voice had sounded like Ben's, but what was he doing here?

Leaning out the still-open door, she saw him and Miles trotting up the gravel drive. Ben waved at her with a grin.

Clutching at her fluttering stomach, she pulled herself back inside the carriage and closed her eyes. Dared she hope that Miles had come to tell her what he hadn't said last night—that he didn't want her to leave, after all?

But surely if he'd meant to make any sort of declaration, he would have come alone. Likely Ben had simply talked him into wishing her and Terry farewell.

Before she could gather her wits, she heard them trudge closer to the door. She peeked out just long enough to take in Ben's flushed complexion and the unreadable expression on Miles' handsome face.

''I feared we would miss you,'' Ben said, his breath coming in puffs. ''Miles has been creeping along at a snail's pace this morning—despite his having a particular reason to hurry.''

''Ben, please.'' Miles glared at his friend, then slid a glance toward Mellie.

She looked down hastily, playing at fixing a ribbon on her reticule. *There is my answer,* she thought. Ben had dragged him along, reluctant even to see her.

"Well, I shall just go and see what Mrs. Burke needs from the village then, shall I?" Ben winked at Mellie.

She caught the gesture out of the corner of her eye. *Miles told him!* Hot embarrassment filled her cheeks.

He walked off, whistling, while she sat, mortified. As for Miles, she couldn't bear looking at him.

After a long moment of silence, he cleared his throat, as if about to speak.

Dreading what he might say, she swallowed and tried to take things in hand by speaking first. "How . . . er, kind of you to see me off. You have caught me rather off guard, however, I fear."

"Mellie, I know this won't mean much to you," he said, speaking rapidly, "but I couldn't let you leave without another attempt to apologize for last night."

His quiet, intimate tone made her lips quiver. She started to lift her gaze again, but he thrust a bouquet of wildflowers through the carriage door. Dazed, she took the haphazard cluster, automatically holding them up to her nose and breathing in their faint, sweet scent. Did this mean he'd changed his mind about the kiss? No, he'd said he wanted to apologize, and an apology was an expression of regret.

"Thank you," she said stiffly.

"As for apologizing, I don't know how—"

"That isn't necessary," she interrupted, mustering up her pride. "You should know by now that I'm not typical of my gender. I suppose you gathered last night that dalliance isn't exactly my forte. Let's forget about our, er, lapse in discretion. You're too important to me as a professional colleague to let this come between us."

He looked doubtful. "But, I . . . I never should have conducted myself so. I know you were upset when you retired last night. If I contributed to your distress—"

"You contributed to my distress by agreeing with

my father about sending me to London now.'' Despite the pain she needed to hide, she looked him squarely in the eye. ''Miles, I thought you, of all people, would understand what the project we're working on means to me. You yourself turned down the opportunity to see Belzoni's exhibition because of your work here. How can you possibly believe that something you deem wrong for you could be right for me?''

''Ho, Miles!'' The booming voice of Sir William broke into their conversation. He stepped up beside Miles and slapped him on the shoulder. ''Nice of you and Ben to come up and see my girls off.''

Miles didn't return her father's smile. He glanced at her, then looked at Sir William. ''I wanted to make sure Mellie knew I'd continue digging for the plate while she's gone.''

The older man nodded. ''Very good.''

She twisted her mouth, hardly placated. ''If you want to continue work on *my* project in my absence, then I'll expect regular progress reports from you.''

''Certainly. I'll write you daily.''

Her eyes widened. No one—especially not a man—had ever written her regularly about anything. She cleared her throat. ''When you near the plate, I shall return to the Park, whether or not the Season is over.''

The two men glanced at each other, then her father turned to her. ''When that time comes, if Miles pleases, he may hold off working further until your return in six weeks, but I cannot have you miss any of your Season.''

''I'll wait,'' Miles said quickly. ''I'll do only enough to reverse yesterday's damage, then I'll help Ben with the mosaic.''

Some of her tension eased. Her project would still be here when she returned—and it sounded as though Miles would, too.

"Commendable of you," her father said.

She thought so, too, but didn't see fit to tell them.

"By the way, Miles, I'd like to get your opinion about something." Sir William dug inside his waistcoat pocket and pulled out a mangled piece of bronze. "Have you ever seen the like of this coin?"

The two stepped aside into better light and bent their heads together. Mellie looked back down at her flowers. Lifting them to her nose again, she found they made a convenient veil to hide behind. She sensed someone watching her and looked up to see Ben at the carriage door again.

He glanced behind him, where Miles spoke with her father. Turning back to her, he pointed to a sealed envelope lodged in amongst her blossoms. "Just in case Miles had no chance to tell you, I thought I should mention that he wrote you a note. He said earlier he hopes you'll open it when Terry isn't around."

"Oh." Once more, heat suffused her face. She had thought she'd evaded any further reference to the kiss, but apparently Miles had been compelled to reiterate his regret in writing. On top of that, here was Ben to remind her that he, too, knew about the incident.

She fingered the missive but didn't pull it out to read. Surely he wouldn't have written anything tender to her.

"He wanted to reassure you about the plate project, I believe," Ben said. "I understand you two had a row about it last night. He didn't say exactly what happened between you, but I can assure you he regrets it today. The man has had a fit of the blue devils all morning."

Miles *hadn't* told him, it seemed. That, at least, offered her some comfort. Bennie could still respect her. Unable to think of a reply, she sat mute.

"I can see you're still angry, and I'll be the first to admit that Miles has been a trial lately. I will say, however, that he's generally a more amiable fellow. If not, I certainly wouldn't share a house with him.''

Terry chose this moment to dash out the front door, saving Mellie the need to respond. Mrs. Burke followed, carrying two hampers of provisions.

As Terry spotted Mellie in the carriage, her face lit up with surprise. She nodded her approval, then turned to Miles and Ben. ''Good morning, gentlemen. Mr. Romney, I believe one of these hampers is intended for you. The other is for our journey.''

As Ben took one basket from the housekeeper, Miles bowed to Terry. ''I wish you a safe and pleasant trip, Lady Moorehead. Enjoy the Season.''

When Ben seconded his wishes, Terry thanked them both. She turned to her father and pecked him on the cheek. *''Au revoir* now, Papa. We'll see you in town soon.''

She took the remaining hamper from Mrs. Burke and climbed into the carriage. As Sir William closed the door and stepped back, she said to him, ''There's no sense in drawing out our farewells, especially since we're running late. Off we go.''

The coach pulled away with everyone waving goodbye. Mellie stole one last glance at Miles. Their gazes locked briefly before Sir William drew his attention elsewhere again.

As the figures in front of the house grew smaller with distance, the knot in Mellie's stomach seemed to grow larger. When the trees lining the drive had completely obstructed her view, she leaned back in her seat, trying not to heed the sickening swaying of the carriage.

Terry eyed her with concern. ''Do try to eat some of Mrs. Burke's bread, dear. A little nibble will help you feel more the thing.''

She lifted the hamper from the floor and placed it

on the opposite bench, next to Miles' bouquet. "Why, how lovely! Where did these flowers come from?"

"They're from Miles . . . and Ben." Not knowing the contents of the note, Mellie prayed her sister wouldn't notice it.

"Wonder of wonders." Terry opened the hamper and broke off a chunk of bread, handing it to her. "I wouldn't have expected such a gesture from those two. Perhaps your archaeological mates actually have noticed you're female."

"Perhaps." Mellie bit off a tiny piece of the bread and chewed it for a ridiculous length of time. She had finally noticed they were male, too—one in particular.

Her sister settled back in the seat and gazed out the window. "How nice it is to look out upon the English countryside again. Of course, there isn't nearly so much color here as in Antigua, but familiarity has a beauty all its own."

Mellie made no reply, concentrating all her efforts on swallowing some sustenance. She listened in silence as the wheels rolled on and Terry made observations about the passing scenery. Eventually, she managed to down the whole chunk of bread and her stomach settled somewhat. By then her sister's head had slumped against the plush cushions of the seat.

"Terry? Are you awake?"

Receiving no response, Mellie quietly snatched the envelope out of Miles' bouquet. She plucked off the wax seal and pulled out the card with fumbling fingers.

Dearest Mellie,
    If at all possible, please find it in your heart to pardon my conduct last night. I wish you all the best in your Season.

                                            Yours, etc.,
                                            St. Leger.

She flipped it over as if expecting more on the back, but naturally it was blank. Blinking back a tear, she stuffed the brief note into her reticule. Why should she feel so disappointed? After all, she'd hardly expected a confirmed bachelor to pay court to her just because of one ill-begotten kiss. Had she?

She stared out at the passing landscape with unseeing eyes, desperately trying to convince herself that she had not. Her work was the important factor in her life. If a handsome face had distracted her from her true purpose, it was only a temporary aberration. She would recover . . . eventually.

With a heart and head equally heavy, she watched the road for some time. At last, the onset of exhaustion blanked everything out with slumber.

Ten

For the third time, Miles reread the report he'd spent most of the evening writing. He'd related every detail of his work that day, and he hadn't even accomplished anything significant. Mellie would read about every move he'd made, right down to calling for her groom's help in clearing away two boulders. On the last page he'd even included a sketch of a large but unremarkable urn excavated that afternoon.

He could think of nothing more to say—nothing except, of course, the matters that had consumed him all week. But naturally he couldn't ask whether or not she'd forgiven him for kissing her—or whether the memory of that moment haunted her the way it did him. He couldn't tell her how much he missed working with her—that he longed to watch her, to have her brush up against him, to catch a whiff of the lavender scent emanating from her hair. . . . The most personal he dared venture was to remark twice that he regretted not having her on hand to offer insight as her project progressed.

He set down the letter and frowned over his preoccupation with her. Tonight he'd actually considered bringing up the Belzoni exhibition and hinting that he'd grown worried he might lament missing it. Yes, part of him even wished she would renew the invitation he'd declined. More likely, she'd tell him to go to blazes. In the week she'd been gone, he'd written her every day and hadn't received a word in return.

"Do you realize how long you've been at that desk?"

The sound of Ben's voice coming from the direction of the door prompted him to look up. His friend leaned against the jamb, one hand on his hip.

Miles knew full well how much time he'd wasted, but he had no desire to be quizzed. Offering no response, he looked back down at his work.

"Over two hours." Ben stepped into the room. "Weren't you and I supposed to ride into the village tonight and stop at the Bull and Adder?"

"I'm finishing up now." Miles stared at the last paragraph he'd written, hoping that if he averted his eyes long enough, his friend would leave.

He had no such luck. Ben flopped down on an over-stuffed armchair in front of the hearth. "If you tarry much longer, the tavern will be closed by the time we get there."

Miles grimaced, picking up his quill and adjusting the nib. "Just let me wind up this letter to Mellie. If I left this obligation hanging over my head, I'd never enjoy myself at the tavern."

Ben sighed and picked up the poker, jabbing at the fire. "I'm a rather indifferent letter writer myself—or so my mother often tells me."

Miles tapped his pen on the inkwell. "I find that correspondence is generally done more quickly when one is left to it alone."

"Oh, I won't bother you. I just want to warm

myself.'' He set the poker back down and held his palms out toward the flames. "Cool night, is it not?"

"This isn't the only room in the house with a fire, you know."

"But it's certainly among the warmest." Ben glanced over his shoulder at him. "I don't blame you for being churlish with all that correspondence to tend to. Is it truly necessary to write her every night? In the past few days, you've had little of interest to relate."

Miles dropped his pen on the desk. "I confess I find the task a trial at the moment."

"I suppose you're still trying to make up for that disagreement you had with her." His friend turned back toward the fire. "If you ask me, you've no reason to worry. I told you she's not the type to hold a grudge."

Miles considered his friend's views, but Ben didn't know the whole story. "Then why hasn't she written me back? You did say you tried to convey to her how sorry I was the morning they left, did you not? I still regret that I didn't get another moment with her."

"Yes, for the tenth time, I told her you were wringing your hands in repentance—and that the strife between you had no doubt stemmed from your sour disposition."

"Oh, thank you for *that* commendation." He shoved his letter aside and folded his arms over his chest.

Ben twisted around in his chair to face him. "Why on earth are you so upset about this incident? I thought you didn't like Mellie anyway."

Miles met his friend's stare and weighed whether to enlighten him at last about what had really happened. But, no, revealing everything would be unfair to Mellie. "I simply don't want a colleague of mine to regret entrusting me with a project. You know how I value my academic reputation."

"Miles, there's a point where meticulous crosses the

line to *ridiculous.*'' Shaking his head, Ben turned back around. ''I'm afraid you reached that point some time ago. I can't understand all this fuss about Mellie's good opinion. Anyone who didn't know you better would swear you had a *tendre* for her.''

A pounding at the front door echoed through the front hall, saving Miles from responding.

Ben sprang from his chair. ''We have a visitor— and not a moment too soon. I'll go and greet the obliging soul.''

As he strode from the room, Miles redirected his attention to his letter. Until now, he'd kept his tone strictly academic. He wondered whether a warmer closing might induce her to reply this time. Of course, he couldn't make the sentiments *too* warm.

Before he had time to work out his phrasing, Ben reappeared with Sir William at his side. Miles stood abruptly to greet the baronet. In the few times they'd met since Mellie's departure, he'd felt uncomfortable, conscious of slighting the man's daughter. Obviously she hadn't told her family about the incident, but that did nothing to ease his conscience.

While Ben offered their guest a choice of seating, Miles fetched a decanter of brandy and three snifters. ''To what do we owe this honor, sir? We've seen little of you this week.''

''That's precisely why I stopped by.'' Choosing the chair Ben had vacated, he sat down. ''I had every intention of helping you with Mellie's project while she's gone, but my tenants have required more of my time than usual. If I'm to visit London in less than a fortnight, as I hope, I've a great deal of estate business to settle before then.''

Miles handed him a brandy and sat down on a sofa across from him. ''Don't give it another thought. The work proceeds slowly but steadily. In fact, I was just now closing a letter to your daughter, detailing today's progress."

"Excellent." Sir William glanced over at the sheets of stationery on the desk. "If one can judge by length, you've written a thorough report. She should be pleased."

Still standing, Ben looked toward the papers, too. "I should say so. There must be three full pages here—and that's only from *today.*"

Miles cleared his throat, embarrassed by his excessive efforts. Trying to stem any questions about how much he'd written, he asked the baronet, "Have you had any word from the ladies yet, sir?"

"Not from Mellie, but I got a letter from Terry today, and she says they're both well. She herself is disappointed with how few acquaintances they have in town—but I don't know what else she expected, when none of our family has kept up with London society. As for Mellie, evidently she's content to drag her maid about to historical attractions every day. I get the impression she's enjoying herself more than she anticipated. Thank goodness. I'd hate to see her miserable on account of my decision to send her into town."

Miles sipped his drink, hoping he didn't look too eager for information. "Did Lady Moorehead happen to mention if Mellie's been wondering about the plate project?"

"No, which surprised me a bit. Has Mellie written to ask *you* about the work?"

He shook his head.

"How could she?" Ben said. "He's written her so much, there's nothing left for her to ask."

Sir William raised an eyebrow and looked more closely at Miles. "You've taken a great interest in this project. You must be convinced the plate she's found is really silver."

"Well, not exactly. That is, the site is, er, interesting regardless. The concentration of artifacts there is so rich that even if something one finds is less than fascinating, there's always another piece to uncover."

The baronet gave him a strange, faint smile. "And so far this week you've found much to report to Mellie?"

He swallowed, wondering if the man suspected his interest wasn't entirely scholarly. "Nothing momentous, but I've made sure to give her detailed descriptions of everything. I wouldn't like to see her ruin her Season pining to be here."

Ben sauntered over to the sofa and sat down beside him. "Mellie's hardly one to pine. She'll make good use of her time, wherever she is. There are plenty of ancient treasures to study in London."

Her father nodded. "I agree—and I believe she'll come to enjoy herself socially, too. She's a beautiful woman, and Terry tells me she's already drawing her share of male attention. Some fortunate fellow is bound to turn her head. I only hope it will be someone I can approve."

Miles frowned. He hadn't given any thought to the men that would be dangling after her in town. With stunning looks and a decent fortune, she'd have city bucks breaking down the door to pay her calls. Furthermore, Euterpe would encourage her to flirt outrageously—assuming Mellie didn't already have the notion herself. In fact, *that* was likely why she hadn't written him. She was too busy dallying!

Ben shrugged. "She's not the sort to choose a husband unwisely, I think."

"I hope not, but women her age can be impetuous." Sir William pulled a packet of tobacco out of his pocket and prepared to fill his pipe. "When Clio and Euterpe made their come-outs, I feared for them at every turn. Mellie seems to have more of a head about her, but I still worry that some young fop will lure her off into a compromising situation.''

Like I did, Miles thought, scowling into his brandy, *and she was willing enough to be lured.*

Ben laughed. ''Mellie would never associate with the kind of coxcomb who would take advantage of her. She'd spot that sort a mile away and make sure she kept her distance. Don't you agree, Miles?''

''Oh, er—'' He cleared his throat. ''I would hope so.''

Sir William looked at him squarely. ''You don't seem as confident about the matter as Bennie. Too bad I can't be in town for nearly another fortnight. A few father-and-daughter outings would show her suitors she has someone looking after her.''

''Do you mean to attend balls and such?'' Ben asked, his distaste apparent in his tone.

''Perhaps one or two—but I have other, more interesting outings planned, too. I've been thinking of taking her to Belzoni's exhibition.''

Miles started. ''Belzoni's exhibition?''

''Yes. The fellow has constructed a recreation of an Egyptian tomb. He's included many authentic artifacts along with the replicas. I read a very favorable account of it in the *Gazette.*''

''I saw the article, too.'' Ben sat up straighter and turned to Miles. ''You and I should ride into London and see it. Who knows when we'll get to the real Egypt?''

Miles' answer stuck in his throat. Such a trip would likely include visiting Mellie, and while part of him wanted to jump at the chance, to do so would be asking for trouble. How would he react if she did indeed have suitors surrounding her? If he were sensible, he'd wish her well with them—but a knot in his stomach suggested he would feel something else.

"Aren't you too engrossed in the mosaic for that?" he managed to ask Ben.

His friend shrugged. "I can spare a couple of days away from the field for an event like this. It's no different from waiting out a rainy spell."

Sir William took a draw on his pipe. "Perhaps you two should take Mellie to the exhibition rather than I. You could go into town sooner than I can and keep an eye on her for a few days. Then I won't worry so much about her before I get there. When I arrive, she and I can find other things to do."

Miles froze. The thought of seeing her excited him, but he feared that after the way he'd treated her she might not want to go anywhere with him. Whether she'd taken offense at his kissing her or because he hadn't defended her work to the others, he had definitely suffered in her opinion. "I'm sure she'd rather go with her father."

The baronet laughed. "No young woman would rather be seen with her father than a couple of young bucks. As for me, I'll be happy to know she's with men I can trust."

Miles cast his gaze downward again, ashamed of himself.

"It'll be our pleasure," Ben said.

"Excellent." Sir William's gaze fell on Miles again. "Why don't you suggest a date in the letter you're writing? That way, she'll know to keep the day open."

He hesitated, still not convinced she'd agree—but he couldn't very well explain that to her father. He gave the man a reluctant nod. "I'll propose the idea to her."

"Splendid. Will you take up residence at your house in Grosvenor Square, or have you let that out for the Season?" Sir William lifted his glass. "I don't suppose it would be appropriate for you to stay with my daughters, but I could ask Euterpe. With her so anxious to expand her social circle, she might relax her usual strictures.''

"No! That is, there's no need. My aunt Atkins is staying in the town house, but she'll insist that Ben and I come to her. She often complains about how infrequently I visit.''

"Good. Then you'll want to be in the city for at least several days. That should please my girls, since they know so few people there. Perhaps you might squire them about to a ball or two. Gaining the notice of an earl couldn't hurt Mellie's social standing.''

Miles took some brandy to try to soothe a dryness in his throat. "No doubt my aunt would like to meet your daughters. I'll ask if she can gain them entry into a few of the better gatherings.''

"Perfect. I appreciate your help—with this and with Mellie's project.'' He drained his snifter and set it down. "I'd best get back to the manor now. Tomorrow I have another long day in store.''

Ben stood. "Let me show you out.''

"Thank you.'' The baronet rose as well.

Miles followed suit but stayed behind when the others walked into the hall. He sat back down at his desk and picked up his pen, debating how to word this proposal. He supposed he'd emphasize that Sir William had suggested the plan—and point out how much the idea excited Ben. Perhaps Ben's coming would quell Mellie's objections to his own presence. With Ben as chaperon, she'd know she would be safe from his advances.

He ran a nervous hand through his hair. What if that wasn't enough to reassure her? If she refused the invitation, how would he ever explain it to her father?

And what if she accepted? Would she act cool toward him but warm toward her entourage of suitors? Or would she return to the tantalizing minx she'd been the week they'd worked together?

He truly didn't know which would be the worse fate for him.

Two days later, Mellie descended the front stairs of the house she and Terry had let in Curzon Street.

"Is that you, love?" her sister called from the parlor.

She reached the main hall and turned into the room. "Indeed, it is."

"Oh, good." Terry lay on an ornate recamier, holding a swatch of needlework close to her face. "I was just about to get up and check on you. Rodney will be here to collect you any minute."

"Actually, I'm running ahead of schedule. I don't expect his lordship for another half hour."

"Don't forget that you have leave to call him by his given name." Terry looked up and eyed Mellie's new gown of vertically striped green-and-gold sarcenet. She smiled. "Very nice. I knew that fabric would do your figure justice—and the bonnet complements the outfit perfectly."

Mellie shrugged and tossed the hat onto a nearby chair.

Her sister pursed her lips. "Can't you show more enthusiasm about this outing? Rodney is handsome, titled, and owns an estate practically next door to Lowery Park. That would suit your desire to be near Father. You could hardly ask for a better prospect, yet before today you twice put off this engagement to see the Tower."

"Well, I'm going today, so there's no more cause for you to complain."

Terry sighed and looked back at her netting. "If

only your disposition matched your fine looks this morning.''

Mellie rolled her eyes. She knew that her new wardrobe had put her in good looks, but it meant little to her when the one person she wanted to impress was nowhere near. Miles had kept his word and written her every day, but his letters were painfully businesslike. He obviously considered her only an associate—just as she'd thought. She still couldn't understand why he'd kissed her the night before she'd left. Evidently he'd drunk more at dinner than she'd realized.

Taking a seat across from her sister, she asked, ''Has the post arrived yet?''

''I have it right here, not that there's anything of interest.'' Terry reached for a silver tray that held several cards and letters. She flipped through the items on top. ''Lady Lytton wrote a note to thank me for visiting her bedside, and we received an invitation to the ball that dreadful Mrs. Moulton is holding. Despite Gwyn's claim that the woman is tolerably well-bred, I remain undecided about whether we should accept.''

''Is there no word from home?''

She shook her head. ''Nothing from Father today— though it appears that St. Leger sent his daily report. I must say I've never known a man to write anyone as diligently as he does you. Men are notoriously poor correspondents. If only he ever penned you a *personal* word, I'd suspect you'd made a conquest.''

Mellie pressed her lips together and took the letter from her. ''We *know* he's a confirmed bachelor.''

Her sister's gaze shot to meet hers. ''Is that a trace of regret I detect in your tone?''

She hesitated, tempted for an instant to confide everything and ask Terry's opinion. But what did her sister's views matter? They wouldn't change the fact that Miles had rejected her. She looked down and pried open the seal. "I never said I was a nun."

"Indeed?" Terry's voice lifted with interest. "Perhaps there's hope for you yet."

"I'm so glad I can amuse you." She unfolded the letter. "Now pray hush so I can skim through this before your wonderful Rodney arrives."

"Very well. I wouldn't want you to make him wait any longer than you already have."

Mellie ignored her, biting her lip as she focused on her name written in Miles' hand. Goodness, he'd sent her *three* pages this time. Though she'd given up hoping he'd allude to anything other than archaeology, she had to concede he was kind to keep her so well informed. He described his findings in such detail she felt as though she were experiencing the work through him. She would have been quite gratified had she still thought of him merely as a colleague. As it was, she nearly cried at the end of each report when he signed off without even a touch of emotion.

"The way you're staring at that, one would think it were a love letter," Terry said. "What has he to say that's so fascinating?"

Mellie shook off her thoughts and began scanning the contents. "Nothing earth-shattering. He's made more progress in the dig. James helped him move some boulders. They found a large storage urn. And . . . oh."

Her sister stopped netting. "What is it?"

She gulped and reread the paragraph more carefully, making sure she'd understood correctly. "Why, he and Bennie are coming into town for an archaeological exhibition . . . and they've invited me to go with them."

Terry set down her needles and looked at her more closely. "What a nice surprise for you."

"Yes." Her heartbeat quickened with the first glimmer of anticipation she'd felt in over a week. "Yes. I can't believe they're coming. He says it was Papa's idea. Hmm. Well, I'll be very pleased to see him— *them*, that is. It'll be nice to have two more acquaintances in town, will it not?''

Her sister smiled but kept her lips together. The expression looked almost sly. She nodded. ''I daresay it will.''

Mellie looked back down, afraid her face would reveal the full extent of her excitement. ''They're going to stay with Miles' aunt, Lady Atkins, in Grosvenor Square. He says he'll introduce us to her.''

''Excellent,'' Terry murmured, the reaction unusually subdued for her. ''What an interesting turn of events this is.''

A knock at the door made both women look up. Mellie set down the letter and stood as the butler ushered in Lord Gough. Thrust into high spirits by the news she'd received, she greeted the viscount with an unfeigned smile.

''A pleasure to see you again, Miss Melpomene.'' He bowed low over the hand she offered. Straightening again, he pushed back a blond lock that had fallen over his striking blue eyes.

''Please, make it Mellie,'' she said.

''Certainly, Mellie. I had trouble identifying you with the Greek muse of tragedy, anyway.''

Terry laughed, finally exerting herself to sit up straight. ''Perhaps our parents should have chosen a happier goddess to name her for, but my father says they fell in love with the sound of *Melpomene*.''

''Oh, I didn't mean to take away from the name.'' Rodney smiled and turned back to Mellie. ''It has a melodic quality that suits you perfectly.''

She grinned. ''If you'd ever heard me on the pianoforte, you wouldn't say so.''

Everyone laughed and she gathered up her things to

go. While Rodney helped her with her spencer, he answered Terry's inquiries about his sister. A moment later, the pair set off.

A beautiful spring day reinforced Mellie's good humor, and her escort seemed as cheerful as she. As they drove across town, he satisfied her questions about his travels and made surprisingly intelligent queries into her pursuits.

At the Tower, they spent hours touring the buildings. Rodney showed as much curiosity as she about the medieval treasures and relics. After a wealth of engaging discussion and exploration, they stopped to rest on a bench on the Green.

"I hope you don't mind my wanting to sit," he said. "You may have noticed walking can be a chore for me. Years ago, a willful stallion threw me, and the hip I broke is here to remind me how foolhardy I once was."

"I'm sorry." She reproached herself for forgetting the limp she'd originally thought a Byronic affectation. That idea seemed foolish now, but she was glad he'd revealed the true cause. After such a pleasant day, her views of him had changed. She got the feeling he was about as different from Gwyn as she herself was from her sisters. "You should have said something sooner. I wouldn't have minded skipping the end of our tour. All of the walking has exhausted me, too."

"Oh, I'm not a complete invalid. I've enjoyed every minute here."

"Me, too." She gave him a shy smile. Until today she couldn't have imagined having such an agreeable outing with a man she barely knew. Perhaps there was less to socializing with the opposite sex than she had feared.

They sat in comfortable silence, watching tourists feed the renowned ravens of the Tower.

"Has our visit lived up to your expectations?" he asked after a while. "I'm interested in hearing a historian's perspective."

She laughed. "I don't dare call myself a historian here. Medieval times are scarcely my forte. Most of the knowledge I have goes back considerably further in time."

"Then perhaps you found the day instructive?"

"Yes, I learned a good deal—and was duly moved by what we saw. Finding oneself in the spot where famed historical figures lost their heads has a strong effect on the senses."

"True." He shook his head. "But I still imagine you must be spoiled for sites like this, being used to places far older."

"Perhaps," she admitted, impressed by his insight. "To be frank, my own little Roman villa does appeal to me more."

"No wonder. The older an artifact is, the more amazing that it has survived. Tell me more about this silver plate you mentioned earlier. How exciting it must be to find something so ancient and valuable."

"To own the truth, it may all come to naught. I like to think I'm on the verge of a fantastic discovery, but my fabulous plate might be nothing more than a rusty old iron shield."

He shook his head. "I suspect you're selling your instincts short. You clearly have a good deal of experience in the field. I'd wager you have good reason to believe the plate is silver."

"Little more than a hunch, though I confess that after all of these years, I've come to take my hunches seriously. If *I* don't, who will?"

He met her gaze squarely, unquestionably absorbed. "Pray share more details with me. Assuming this plate would have been used as a serving dish, did you find it in a dining room? Did the ancient Romans even have dining rooms?''

"The wealthier ones did, and our villa would have indeed belonged to someone well off. Oddly enough, however, the plate is buried outside the walls. I can't say why. Perhaps someone buried it there for safekeeping—or maybe a servant stole the piece and hid it, planning to recover it later.''

"Given the location, 'tis remarkable you found it at all. Do you and your father do much digging outside the walls?''

"We haven't yet. As of now, there's only one other outside pit besides the trench where the plate lies— but that's only because we've had so much to occupy us within the walls.''

He shook his head. "Piecing together parts of the past must give you a great sense of satisfaction. If I'm not being too presumptuous, do you think my sister and I might sometime prevail on Sir William to show us around the ruins?''

"Certainly." She smiled, pleased by his eagerness. The thought occurred to her that he had such an easy manner he might provide a buffer for her when she saw Miles again. "In fact, if you'd like to hear more about the villa, the two archaeologists currently visiting the Park are coming to London early next week. Would you like to meet them?''

His shoulders slumped. "I'm afraid I have a business journey scheduled then.''

"Oh." She actually felt disappointed. Not only would Rodney have detracted notice from how nervous she was likely to be, he would have shown Miles that *some* men found her intriguing.

"Perhaps you and I can get together again before I leave town," he said. "I'm sure there's much more about archaeology that you could teach me.''

"That would be a pleasure." She was always glad for another opportunity to discuss her favorite topic, and her seeing him again would please Terry, too— not that she thought of him as a suitor. He was a pleasant enough companion, but she couldn't imagine ever feeling more for him than that.

They continued discussing the villa while he drove her home. Before they parted, they agreed on a date for their engagement.

When she entered the town house, she found Terry had gone out, so she went to her chamber. Catching her reflection in the mirror, she marveled again at her new elegance. Her outward sophistication, combined with the surprisingly smooth outing, had restored some of her confidence. Not once during her time with Rodney had she felt awkward or inexperienced, she realized.

She stepped closer to the mirror, telling herself she'd have to remember this feeling when Miles arrived and began to unnerve her. Perhaps her naïveté had shown when he'd kissed her, but a woman wasn't expected to have *that* sort of experience, was she? She was no expert on social customs, but she didn't believe a gentleman was supposed to take such liberties unless he had serious intentions. On an equal playing field— in Bennie's company, or in her sister's—she would show Miles she could comport herself with grace. Why, Rodney obviously liked her well enough, and he seemed a man of the world. According to Terry, other men in town were showing interest in her, too.

She hoped Miles would see evidence of that when he arrived. Despite her distaste for "missish" thinking, she couldn't help but wish he'd come to regret rejecting her.

Eleven

"I can't believe I let you drag me out of the house again so soon after that long ride from Dorset." Ben slumped against the backrest on the box of Miles' carriage. "Lady Atkins must think we're mad, dashing out into the city streets after scarcely a half hour with her."

Beside him, Miles sat alert at the reins, guiding the horses through London traffic. "She'll understand. When I wrote to tell her we were coming to town, I mentioned Mellie's project and how I've been reporting my progress to her. Naturally, we're eager to see our colleague."

"*You* are, you mean," his friend said. "I could have easily waited till tomorrow. Mellie doesn't even expect us until then."

He drew in a deep breath, struggling not to appear *too* anxious. She had finally written back to him to accept his invitation, but her note had been short and formal. For days he'd been wondering how she would respond to him in person. Now he couldn't bear to wait any longer. "Well, *she* is likely on tenterhooks waiting to discuss her project. She has no one here in town to talk to about her work.''

Ben shrugged. "Assuming she hasn't met other archaeologists during all of those excursions Sir William told us she's been taking."

Miles let the remark go, unable to think of an argument. He hoped one wasn't necessary.

Within a few minutes they turned onto Curzon Street. As he began searching for the address, his heartbeat quickened. Getting so excited about seeing Mellie was ridiculous, he realized. How had he let his attraction to her get so out of hand?

He took a deep breath and tried to steady his nerves. *Absence makes the heart grow fonder,* the old saying went. Perhaps their separation had distorted his perspective, and seeing her would bring him back to his senses. Surely he must have built up her attractions in his mind over the past two weeks. He could only hope that in person her flaws would stand out and snap him out of this alarming infatuation.

He spotted the house, a modest but neat brownstone, and pulled up in front. "We're here, Ben, so now you can stop complaining."

"Good." Ben opened the door and stepped down onto the street. "The sooner this is over, the better. All I want to do for the rest of the day is eat a good dinner and retire early."

Miles joined him on the sidewalk and tied up the horses. They climbed the front steps and knocked at the door. The unfamiliar manservant who took their cards showed them into a small but elegantly appointed drawing room.

"Miles Kennestone, Lord St. Leger, and the Honorable Mr. Benjamin Romney," the man announced.

Lady Moorehead rose from a sofa, setting down a novel she'd been reading. The wide smile she gave them looked genuine. "Welcome to London, gentlemen. I'm so pleased to see you."

The warmth in her greeting surprised Miles. He bowed over her outstretched hand. "And we you, my lady."

She gave Ben her hand next, then gestured for them to sit. "What a pleasant surprise. You're a day early, are you not? When did you arrive in town?"

"We've not been in the city for more than an hour, if you can credit that." Ben leaned back in his chair, extending his legs and crossing them at the ankles. "Miles figured your sister must be on tenterhooks waiting to discuss her project."

"Oh, really?" Euterpe gave Miles a funny, small smile. "Normally I'm sure she would be, but she had an important engagement this afternoon."

"An engagement?" His whole body seemed to sink with disappointment, the force of which surprised him. "You mean to say she's not here?"

"I'm afraid she's been out all morning. She may profess to be an introvert, but she's certainly enjoying an active social life here in London."

Ben raised his eyebrows. "Well, Sir William will be glad to hear that. He was worried about her having a difficult time."

"Yes." Euterpe glanced at a letter lying on a table beside her. "He wrote to tell me how relieved he was that you two would be here to look after us for a few days—not that such vigilance will be necessary. We'll be pleased to see you, of course, but you mustn't feel you have to dance attendance on us. Mellie has plenty of suitors doing that already."

Miles frowned. "What sort of engagement does she have today?"

"An outing with one of her gentlemen friends, naturally.'' She grinned at him. ''A favorite of hers, I think. This is the third time they've been out in a week.''

A sick feeling welled up inside of him. He twisted his mouth, trying not to let the tumult he felt show in his face.

''Indeed?'' Ben asked. ''I never would have expected her to show interest in a man so quickly. Is this fellow an eligible *parti?*''

Euterpe nodded. ''A viscount, as a matter of fact. And he happens to be the brother of one of my friends, so I am doubly pleased by the match.''

''What 'match'?'' Miles demanded. ''Surely she hasn't already accepted an offer from this . . . this person?''

She shrugged. ''Not that I know of, but at the rate they're going, it shouldn't take long for him to reach the sticking point. Three engagements in one week may not seem like a great deal, but Mellie isn't one to spend time with someone unless she truly enjoys the company.''

''Too true.'' Ben laughed. ''The only question that remains is whether the fellow has an interest in archaeology. I suspect he must, if Mellie's partial to him.''

Euterpe tapped her chin, apparently considering the question. ''Well, I don't know if the answer would have been the same a month ago, but he's undoubtedly shown interest lately. She told me he's asked for a tour of the ruins at Lowery Park as soon as possible.''

Ben nodded in approval. ''Sounds promising.''

''I thought so, too.'' She smiled—then glanced around the room as if recalling something. ''Oh, dear, I haven't offered you gentlemen refreshments. After your journey, I imagine you could use something heartier than a plate of scones. Shall I see what Cook has on hand?''

''Thank you, but we can't stay long,'' Ben said. ''I

fear if we did, I'd be in danger of falling asleep in front of you.''

"Are you expecting Mellie back soon?" Miles asked, then winced at his anxious tone. He wondered if Euterpe sensed anything of his feelings. Ben never seemed to pick up on the conflict he'd been having over Mellie, but women had better instincts for that sort of thing.

She held up her hands in a helpless gesture. "Last time those two went out, they were gone most of the day, I'm afraid."

"That settles it then." Ben stood and stretched out his arms, cracking his knuckles. "Please tell her we're sorry we missed her."

"Do you know if she has plans tomorrow?" Miles asked, still seated.

"Why? Are you thinking of going to the exhibit then?"

"Well, yes," he said before Ben could tell her they hadn't yet discussed a time for it. "I'm eager to see what Belzoni has in store for us."

"I'll be sure to let her know." Euterpe stood, prompting him to follow suit. "Perhaps if she's planned something already, she can rearrange her schedule. I don't suppose you'll be in town long, will you?"

Ben shook his head. "Just a few—"

"We haven't decided how long yet," Miles broke in. "But, yes, please tell her we'd like to see the exhibition tomorrow morning."

"Maybe *afternoon*, Miles?" Ben suggested. "I didn't sleep all that well last night."

Miles gave him a dour look. "Morning would be better. We'll want to beat the crowds."

"Of course." Euterpe gave him a crooked grin, apparently amused by their bickering. "And you wouldn't want to give Mellie's suitors a chance to get here first and tempt her to go elsewhere with them, would you?''

He frowned, wondering whether she did see through him and was teasing him now. But the coquette in her might just as easily come forth on her sister's behalf without prodding. Either way, he didn't dare answer, afraid that if he did his jealousy would ring out loud and clear.

Her gaze weighed on him heavily. ''Don't worry. It's just this one fellow who's likely to tempt her. As I said, she seems to have singled him out as her favorite.''

He set his jaw, his aggravation mounting. How had he let himself reach this point? Perhaps he should have insisted on remaining at Lowery Park, reminding himself that he could live without Mellie. Here, he didn't feel so certain. He knew for sure that he didn't want that upstart viscount to have her. Did he actually want her for himself?

Unable to bear her sister's scrutiny any longer, he looked down to pull on his gloves. ''We'd best go. Ben's exhausted.''

''Mellie will be sorry she missed you,'' she said. ''I'll do the best I can to make sure she's here tomorrow morning when you arrive. Shall we say ten o'clock?''

''That'll be fine.'' Miles turned toward the hall.

She walked with them to the door, Ben handling most of the farewells while Miles simmered in jealousy and self-doubt. While the others tarried on the doorstep, he continued out to the carriage. Untying the horses, he got the gig ready and waited for his friend.

In a few minutes, Ben climbed up beside him on the box. He waved to Euterpe as they pulled away, then leaned back in his seat. ''How about that, Miles? Who would have thought Mellie would have a serious suitor after so short a time in London? She's even piqued the fellow's interest in archaeology.''

He snorted, staring ahead at the road. ''In other words, the lackwit is playing at sharing her interests in order to ensnare her. I can't believe she's falling for such a trick. If nothing else, I thought Mellie had a brain in her head.''

''Pardon?'' His friend turned to look at him. ''Terry gave us no reason to believe this fellow is a lackwit or a conniver. On the contrary, she made her regard for him apparent.''

''Yes, well, *she* would like him.'' He gritted his teeth. ''I'm sure she'd love to get Mellie prudently married off before she has a chance to think twice.''

Ben scratched his head. ''Well, I suppose Terry might be a bit impatient to have her sister settled. You likely didn't hear, but she just confided to me that she hopes *our* presence in London will spur this viscount into action. Can you imagine being positioned as the fellow's rival?''

He steeled his gaze on the road. ''Possibly.''

His friend shot a look at him. ''What? Oh, you mean it could be a lark. Maybe you're right. I can just picture Mellie's face if *we,* her respected colleagues, were to start lavishing attention on her, like a couple of love-struck striplings. She'd be mortified. . . . Say, can we stop at Gunter's on the way back to Grosvenor Square?''

Miles shook his head to himself. Ben's density in some matters was astounding, considering his intelligence in scholarly areas. He supposed there was no use enlightening him and asking him for advice. ''I don't think so. All of our travel is beginning to wear on me, too, now.''

''Oh, come on. I haven't had one of their ices in ages.''

"Very well, if you insist." He made a turn in the direction of the confectioner's shop. "But don't expect me to make conversation while we're there. I'm no longer in the mood for talking."

"What luck that you were available this afternoon," Rodney said to Mellie, as he drove his phaeton through Hyde Park.

"Yes, I'm glad that you dropped by." She gazed at the sunlit greenery surrounding them and felt as much satisfaction as possible under the circumstances. In truth, she'd hesitated to come out for this drive. Anticipation of Miles' arrival tomorrow had her so distracted, she couldn't imagine making small talk today. Now she was glad that Terry had urged her to get out of the house. Rodney seemed content to pose questions and accept her vacant replies—and this way she got *some* enjoyment from the beautiful day instead of pacing the floors inside.

She spotted a pair of lovers in a passing barouche gazing into each other's eyes. A pang of longing stabbed at her. Had she any chance of ever finding love? She and Miles would have been such a perfect match. Why couldn't he seem to see it?

Looking down into her lap, she bit her lip. Was there anything she could possibly do to change his mind while he was in town? She wondered again whether to consult her sister but wasn't sure she valued Terry's advice enough to bother. Since coming to London, Terry had put all of her energy into garnering invitations, and so far had achieved little. If her expertise with men lay on a similar par to her other social skills, there was no point in seeking it.

"You look as though you're miles away," Rodney

said. "And I think I know you well enough to have a good idea where you fancy yourself: Lowery Park."

She tried to smile but didn't quite succeed. "Perhaps, but I hope you're not offended. I'm enjoying our drive, but I'll always have reason to wish I were home."

"I understand. You're anxious to uncover your Roman plate." He directed the horses through a patch of congestion on Rotten Row. "Aren't your associates arriving in town soon? Having them here to discuss the villa should offer you some diversion."

Whether it would or would not she couldn't say, but that had nothing to do with her work. She forced her thoughts back to the current discussion. "They'll be here tomorrow. Are you sure you won't be able to meet them?"

"Unfortunately, I'll be setting off tomorrow."

"So soon?" she asked, only vaguely interested. She might miss Rodney's companionship after Miles and Ben went home again, but with so much on her mind now it was hard to care. "Will you be gone for long?"

"A week at the most. I'll be back in town for the end of the Season."

"Oh, good." She stared off at a cluster of trees along the road.

"I see you're still preoccupied with your project. Has your colleague written with more word on his progress?"

"Indeed. From what he says, there's little left to do except extract the plate."

"How exciting." He turned toward her, grinning with obvious enthusiasm. "The plate is just sitting there waiting for you to take it?"

She sighed. "Pretty much . . . if only my father would let me come home."

Their conversation lagged for a moment while he maneuvered through a dense patch of traffic. When they'd passed the swarm, he looked toward her again. "Say, I know what might cheer you up. Why don't we stop at Gunter's for ices? I judge the weather warm enough. Don't you?"

She made an effort to smile. "For me, it's always warm enough for ices."

"I thought you might say that." He directed the horses out of the park.

They rode in silence for another five minutes, then pulled up in front of the confectioner's.

"Lord, this place is a crush," he said. "I'd hate to drag you through the masses only to find we cannot be seated."

"We can skip the ices, if you like. I can do without."

"No, I wouldn't dream of it. Oh, here's a stroke of luck. I see Mrs. Moulton and her little ones on their way out." He waved to a woman wearing a garish deep green satin gown and a matching hat bedecked with an orange plume.

She spotted him and smiled widely, steering her two young boys toward the phaeton. "How do you do, my lord? Such a pleasure to see you."

He nodded. "Likewise, Mrs. Moulton. Allow me to introduce you to Miss Melpomene Lowery, sister to your old school chum, Lady Moorehead. Miss Lowery, Mrs. Winifred Moulton."

Mellie bobbed her head.

The woman dropped a deep curtsy. "A pleasure indeed. I've heard so much about you, I feel I know you already."

Rodney smiled broadly. "It's about time the two of you met in person. I know Miss Lowery was disappointed when she was unable to attend your ball the other night. I wonder, Mrs. Moulton, would you be so good as to keep her company while I dash inside to inquire about a table? I promise I shall only be a moment.''

"But, of course. I shall be delighted at the chance to get to know Miss Lowery a little.''

"Wonderful.'' He turned to Mellie. "If nothing is available, I'll give my name and we can stop back later.''

"Hurry back,'' she said, watching him climb down from the phaeton. She looked at Mrs. Moulton with a weak smile, just as the woman's older child, a husky boy of about four, chose to run down the pavement after a stray dog.

"Edmund! Edmund, come back here now!''

When the boy continued chasing the cur, his mother scurried after him, the smaller child bouncing in her arms.

Mellie sighed and glanced back toward the confectioner's but saw no sign of Rodney. She was about to look away when two familiar faces emerged from the throng in the shop. As they approached, she confirmed it was her colleagues. She stood up in the phaeton, smiling and waving. "Miles! Ben!''

They stopped in their tracks, both looking surprised, then Ben rushed forward with a grin. "Well, hello, Mellie. Fancy meeting you here. We were just by Curzon Street to see you.''

"You were? How sorry I am that I missed you. I didn't expect you until tomorrow.'' She shook his hand, beaming, but when she turned to Miles, her smile withered. He stood with his arms crossed over his chest and the darkest expression she had ever seen him wear. She let her outstretched hand drop to her side.

He gave her a rigid bow. "I trust you're enjoying your stay in London.''

She nodded, studying his countenance with a sinking stomach. He gave her a decidedly forced smile, and she thought her heart would break. Obviously, he took no pleasure in seeing her again. She wondered why he'd even agreed to her father's idea that he and Bennie take her to Belzoni's exhibit. No way to decline without looking rude, she supposed.

"What's the matter with you, Miles?" Ben asked. He turned to Mellie, his brow furrowed. "The journey from Dorset is catching up with him. He was in perfectly good humor earlier."

She cast her gaze downward. So he'd been happy until seeing her. Aloud, she said, "Traveling does erode one's disposition."

"We hear you've been keeping busy," Ben said, a funny smile tugging at his lips. "Terry says you've become a social butterfly."

"Oh, hardly. I mean, for *me,* perhaps, but not by *ton* standards." She moistened her lips. "I'm waiting for a friend to get us a table now. Will you come back inside to join us for a few moments?"

"We can't," Miles said abruptly. "My aunt's expecting us for tea, and I confess I *have* grown fatigued in the last hour. We were hoping, however, to attend the exhibition tomorrow morning—provided you are not too busy?"

She thought she detected a hint of disdain in his voice. Her chances with him were even worse than she'd feared. "Of course I'm not too busy to spend time with you. Nothing is more important to me than my archaeological pursuits."

He met her gaze with a grim look. "Nothing?"

His expression looked so serious, she felt compelled to answer him literally. "In a manner of speaking. Naturally, the people I love are more important to me than a field of science."

"I thought so. In that case, are you still certain you'll be free tomorrow morning?"

She frowned in confusion. "I shall be free all day."

"Then we'll call for you at ten. Until then, I bid you good day." He bowed again and turned away.

Ben watched his friend with wide eyes, then looked at her with a shrug. "I apologize for him, Mellie. No doubt he'll be more himself tomorrow and regret the way he behaved today. But now I'd better catch up with him. I'll see you tomorrow."

He ran off before she could respond—fortunately for her, as tears were welling up in her eyes. Not only had Miles come to town solely for the exhibition, he seemed barely able to stand her company. There was no hope for her.

She spotted Mrs. Moulton returning with both sons in tow. Sniffing, she swiped away her tears. All she could do was try to save face—and the same went for tomorrow, too. She refused to let Miles know how much he'd hurt her. If she did, she'd never be able to face him again when she got home.

Swallowing, she lifted her chin. She would show him that she didn't need him. Tomorrow morning, she would dress in her finest, hold her head up, and discuss archaeology with the utmost intelligence. As far as he was concerned, she'd been having a wonderful time here without him—and would continue now that he'd arrived.

Twelve

"Great frock," Ben said to Mellie as the three of them left the Curzon Street town house the next morning. "It looks like something an Egyptian goddess would wear."

"Exactly what I thought when I saw the pattern in the modiste's book." She looked down at her sheer pleated overdress, tied with a gold ribbon just under her breasts. Beneath this transparent gauze creation, she wore a soft white linen sheath with the lowest cut bodice she'd ever dared sport. She loved the overall effect so much that she was enjoying surprisingly high spirits this morning.

She glanced at Miles to see if he'd taken in her appearance. He looked away quickly, but not before she noticed that his gaze had rested on her breasts. Warm pleasure filled her cheeks. Perhaps he wasn't *entirely* insusceptible to her. Perhaps kissing her hadn't totally repulsed him.

"It suits you," he said stiffly, "and our outing today."

"I'm glad you think so." She thanked her stars

that he wasn't still scowling this morning. He looked serious but not tense, as he had the day before.

They descended to the street. The sun was shining, and the men had ridden in an open phaeton. All three in the party squeezed onto the front bench, with Mellie seated in the middle.

As Miles prompted the horses to take off, the carriage went over a bump, and her thigh grazed his. Feeling the warmth of his body reminded her of the few moments he had held her—how alive he'd felt against her. She peered at his profile through the corners of her eyes and longed to taste his mouth again.

He turned to catch her looking at him. Determined not to appear timid, she forced herself not to look away. She gave him a wavering smile. He hesitated, then returned one of a similar nature.

"I read that Belzoni has an authentic sarcophagus here," Ben said, his tone excited. "Apparently, the man has been all over the Valley of the Kings in Egypt. Lord, I envy him. Do you suppose he might be present today? I could think of a thousand questions to ask him."

"Not likely," Miles said, his gaze back on the road, "but perhaps an assistant of his will be on hand. I'd love to hear exactly where they located this sarcophagus and if they have any idea who was buried in it."

As they drove across town, Ben spoke about the article he'd read in *The Gazette* and speculated about various details. The others chimed in with their own musings. By the time they reached the building where the exhibit was housed, they were caught up in a lively discussion about the latest efforts to decipher ancient Egyptian hieroglyphics. The ease with which Mellie and Miles were talking to each other left her almost giddy with relief. His mood had brightened noticeably, too.

When they stepped down from the phaeton, her blood quickened even more. How exciting it was to tour an accurate model of an Egyptian tomb. According to Ben, Belzoni professed to have seen hundreds of them in person. She looked forward to imagining she was stepping into the past.

Once they'd paid their admission and reached the correct room, they queued up behind a dozen other attendees. Some ten yards ahead, they could see the entrance to the "tomb," a huge wooden structure shaped vaguely like a pyramid and painted to resemble stone. Two burning torches flanked the dark opening in the center, and someone inside made a howling noise at regular intervals.

"Spooky," Mellie said, grinning up at Miles.

He smiled back down at her. "Don't worry. If necessary, I'll protect you."

While they shared a laugh, Ben cleared his throat behind them.

"This is like a circus," he said with disgust. "That monstrosity is the most ill-shaped pyramid I've ever seen. I certainly hope Belzoni took more care in how he displayed the artifacts inside."

The patrons ahead of them in line, however, didn't seem to mind the lack of authenticity. As they drew closer, a particularly loud howl drew a squeal from several ladies in the crowd. The men accompanying them took their arms, leaning down to whisper reassurances in their ears.

Mellie laughed, too excited to disparage the women for their missish behavior—perhaps even understanding it with Miles standing just behind her, making her own heart race. More people had queued up after them, and now the rear of the line began to press forward. She could feel the warmth of Miles' chest at her back, whenever his body brushed up against hers.

They drew closer to the entrance, and another loud howl blared from the tomb. She jumped and grabbed on to his arm. Afterward, she giggled at herself but didn't let go of him. He laughed, too, and covered her hand with his as if to calm her.

She closed her eyes for an instant, savoring the warmth of his fingers, large yet tender and comforting.

"This is asinine," Ben said. "What is that howling supposed to represent? Are we to infer that jackals commonly make their dens in Egyptian tombs?"

"I believe we're supposed to think a resurrected mummy is wailing at us." Mellie smiled over his unwillingness to suspend disbelief. "It's silly but fun, don't you think?"

"No, I think it's misleading to people who don't know any better." Ben pointed at the walls around them as the entered the model tomb. "Look at these hieroglyphs. They're very poorly executed. And what's that in the corner? 'Belzoni' spelled out in capital letters, like so much graffiti. Apparently, *some* archaeologists have no sense of humility."

Miles leaned close to her and whispered, "And some no sense of humor."

She giggled.

Advancing through the first passageway, they turned into an unlit hall. Complete darkness loomed around the next corner. A howl sounded next to her ear, and she yelped, automatically pulling Miles closer. This time she continued to cling to him, laughing. As they stepped into blackness, he wrapped an arm around her shoulders. She leaned her head against his chest, not caring if the move was a bit forward. His heart beat at her ear.

God help her, she wanted to stay right here forever.

"Some exhibition," Ben muttered, invisible in the dark. "We can't see a bloody thing."

The queue continued shuffling forward, pressing her and Miles together. They rounded another bend, and a faint light appeared—another torch. As they neared it, Mellie made out that a larger room lay ahead, likely where the sarcophagus sat.

She twisted to grin up at Miles, and he smiled back at her. With her halfway turned around toward him like this, they were practically embracing. As they stared at each other, their smiles slowly faded. His gaze slid to her lips. *He wants to kiss me,* she thought, her head reeling with excitement.

"What the hell are you doing, Miles?" Ben demanded.

They were no longer in the dark, she realized.

Miles' arm slipped from around her. "Mellie was, er, startled back there. I was just, uh, guiding her through the dark."

Ben frowned. "Perhaps your guidance is not the best sort. Come on, Mellie. Take my elbow."

He offered her his arm, and she placed her hand on it gingerly. The heat of a blush crept up her cheeks, and she hoped the dim light hid it from him. To be caught dallying like a schoolgirl by a respected colleague embarrassed her—but, despite herself, she couldn't completely regret the indiscretion. Had she behaved with cool professionalism, she never would have learned that Miles still had any urge to kiss her.

Recalling the intense look in his eyes made her dizzy, almost ecstatic. Their first kiss couldn't have been a complete disaster, after all. For one moment, at least, he'd been willing to try it again. He still felt some measure of attraction for her, however little. Perhaps she could increase it with the right encouragement— whatever that might be.

For the rest of the tour, she had difficulty paying attention, in spite of her fascination with ancient Egypt.

She did linger at the sarcophagus, in awe of the intricate carvings. Ben was right; the recreations out front were crude at best. Apart from this piece, however, there were few genuine artifacts on display. Every once in a while, she glanced at Miles, but he never met her gaze again, likely avoiding it.

She frowned as they approached the exit of the tomb. No doubt he again regretted the lapse of formality between them. What could she do to swell his interest in her? Perhaps she would seek Terry's counsel, after all. She could always temper her sister's views with her own level head. Besides, she had no one better to consult.

As they stepped outside of the building, she let go of Ben and sighed. *What was Bennie thinking now?* she wondered. Had he been shocked by how she and Miles had behaved in the dark? Would the ride home be awkward now?

"What a load of nonsense," he said, addressing both of them. He had no trouble meeting their gazes and showed no other sign of uneasiness. "I'm going to write to Belzoni and tell him what I think of his so-called tomb. Come on. Let's get out of here. To think that we rode all the way to London for this!"

As soon as the men had seen Mellie home and climbed back up into the phaeton, Ben gave Miles a hard look. "What on earth did you think you were doing back there at the exhibit? You have a fine way of repaying Sir William for his hospitality to us. I can't believe you took advantage of Mellie—a woman too inexperienced to defend herself from a rogue like you."

"Inexperienced? Ha!" Somewhat confounded by his behavior himself, Miles took up the reins and signaled the horses to start. "That woman is a practiced coquette, much like her sisters but more subtle—dangerously so. I've fallen prey to her arts once before, and I fell to them again today.''

Ben gaped at him. ''Are you out of your mind? Mellie's no coquette. I've spent every summer with her for the past six years, and I've never seen her flirt with anyone.''

Miles steered the horses around a corner, his gaze focused on traffic. ''You, my friend, are oblivious to women's wiles. Likely she's tried to use her tricks on you yourself, but with you they don't work.''

A moment of silence ensued, then Ben asked, ''And what tricks did she use on you today?''

He grimaced, uncomfortable at having to explain just what had happened. '' 'Tis hard to recall exactly how she reeled me in. First she came out dressed in that provocative little drapery. During the drive to the exhibit, she kept brushing up against me. Then she squealed over all of those little gimmicks Belzoni had set up to frighten people. The deeper we got into the exhibit, the more she clung to me.''

''So what? Everything you've cited sounds like natural female behavior.''

''Right. Behavior they *naturally* use to entice us men.''

''You're mad.'' Ben crossed his arms over his chest and turned away from him. ''If Mellie had any interest in enticing men, she'd be thrilled to be here in London for the Season. Instead she barely puts up with it. You witnessed how little she wanted to come into town at all. Sir William had to order her here. And today I heard her mention at least twice how much she longs to be home.''

Miles frowned. She *had* said that today—and perhaps even meant it, in part—but she seemed to be enjoying herself enough in London, too. One point, in particular, ate at him. "If she's so artless when it comes to men, how do you explain this beau she's collected in just two weeks? She must be doing something to encourage him."

His friend shrugged. "If she is, she's likely serious about the fellow, as her sister says."

"Then why was she clinging to *me* today?" He snapped the reins, inadvertently quickening the horses. "And why did she let me kiss her the night before she left Lowery Park?"

A stunned silence hung in the air between them.

Miles slowed the gig again and cleared his throat. "Perhaps we should stop somewhere and talk."

"Definitely." Ben's voice sounded grim.

He drove around the corner to Hyde Park and turned the carriage into the entrance. Pulling to the side, he stopped and let the horses graze.

"You kissed Mellie?" Ben asked.

"Mmhmm." He gazed down at his lap. "And she kissed me back, too, I tell you."

Another moment passed while Ben absorbed this information. At last he asked, "Is this what led to the confrontation you two had that night?"

"It *was* the confrontation. Nothing more passed between us. I never even got to apologize properly. As soon as I came to my senses and drew away from her, Euterpe interrupted us on the terrace."

Ben turned to face him. "So what—you simply let Mellie leave for London with no declaration of your feelings?"

"I didn't know what my feelings were."

"Oh, Miles."

"I still don't." He threw his hands up in disgust. "You act as though this matter is all so simple, but I've had women trying to ensnare me since the moment I inherited my title. Widows ten years my senior, voracious mamas with daughters to peddle ... Mellie's own sisters had a go at me last time I stayed at Lowery Park. It stands to reason that she's merely taking her turn at me now. How can I possibly accept that?''

Ben shook his head. "You still believe she's been trying to hoodwink you, after she left the Park and didn't write you for weeks—even though you practically penned her a novel every night? A clever way to lure you in, that. I suppose you think she's a master hand at being coy. But what exactly is *your* game? I've never heard of lavishing attention upon an unwanted admirer in order to drive her away.''

Miles stared at him. Finally he sighed and put a hand up to his brow. "No. I'm beginning to see that the only person I was fooling was myself.''

"So you are serious about her?''

He took a deep breath, then nodded. "I'm afraid so. Am I a fool? She is clearly encouraging that viscount while she dallies with me.''

Ben rubbed his chin in thought. "You likely brought that on yourself when you didn't declare yourself before she left the Park. She may well still be attracted to you, but after your negligence she must doubt your good intentions. Then some upstart viscount came along and showered her with attention. I daresay you drove her into the fellow's arms.''

"Good Lord. Can you be possibly right?'' He kneaded his forehead. His friend's theory was feasible, he acknowledged. "Now what do I do?''

"Get her out of London immediately—away from your rival, before he does any more damage, such as ask her to marry him. Take her back to Lowery Park, where you have the advantage.''

"Now? Against Sir William's wishes?''

"He only wants to see his daughter settled with a

man who will take care of her." Ben met his gaze squarely. "Are you prepared to help him with that?"

Miles thought about the question and nodded, surprised at his conviction once he'd reached it. "Now if I can only talk her into leaving town when her father expressly forbade it."

"I have a feeling she'll jump at any chance to get back to her project." Ben leaned back in the seat and crossed his legs. "Drive her back tomorrow. I'll stay on a few days and catch a post chaise home."

"Are you sure? That will be an inconvenience."

"Not as much an inconvenience as suffering your company if you don't win Mellie over, I think. Ever since we arrived at the Park, you've been a bear to deal with. Now I think I understand why."

He nodded slowly, his mind racing off in other directions. "Sorry."

"Don't mention it."

As he gathered up the reins to leave, Ben shook his head, a smile touching his lips. "I can't believe how cagey you've been about this matter. Imagine all of this going on right under my nose, and I had no idea."

Despite the turmoil in his head, Miles rolled his eyes. "Yes, imagine that."

But as he drove out of the park, he realized he could hardly condemn Ben for his lack of perception. Until now he himself hadn't understood what had been going on in his own heart for the last few weeks.

He urged the horses to pick up the pace. Now that his friend had helped him see straight, he knew what he wanted. His suspicions that Mellie had lured him into her arms had disappeared—but another, deeper fear replaced them: What if he'd abused her trust in him too much and he couldn't win her back from her viscount?

The thought frightened him more than anything ever

had before. He swallowed and set his jaw. At least now he had his head about him and was prepared to fight for her—prepared for the fight of his life.

"I'll drop you off at my aunt's and go back to Curzon Street," he told Ben.

His friend grinned and slapped him on the back. "I'll have a servant start packing your things. Best of luck."

Thirteen

As Miles reached for the knocker on the door at the house in Curzon Street, he heard a carriage pull up behind him. Glancing over his shoulder, he saw Euterpe sitting in the back of a barouche, gathering up parcels. She was obviously just returning from a shopping trip.

"Blast it," he muttered to himself. He couldn't propose taking Mellie back to Lowery Park with her sister listening. Euterpe would unquestionably give him a battle.

"Ho, Miles," she called as she stepped down from the gig. She gave him a warm smile.

"Good day, Lady Moorehead." He turned around and hurried back down the steps to reach for her packages. "Let me take these for you."

"Why, thank you." She handed him the parcels and led him back up to the door. "Were you coming or going? I thought your visit to the exhibition would have ended ages ago."

"It did. That is, Ben and I dropped Mellie off about an hour ago, but I came back to discuss something else with her."

"Oh?" She lifted her eyebrows, but looked away to turn the doorknob.

"Yes—er, something about her project."

"I see." She stepped into the foyer, and a butler appeared to gather up her wrap. After she directed the man to take the packages from Miles as well, she gestured toward the drawing room. "Well, go in and have a seat, Miles. My sister must be upstairs. I'll see if she's available."

"Thank you, my lady." He went in while Euterpe began her climb to the second floor. Too nervous to sit, he paced the perimeter of the room, examining the architecture and the smattering of paintings on display.

After a few minutes, he heard soft footsteps descending the stairs. Mellie entered the room, a faint crease forming at the top of her nose. She still wore the elegant classical style gown she'd had on earlier—but she'd since taken her hair down and looked even more beautiful now. "Hello, Miles. Terry told me you were here. Is everything all right?"

"Quite." He stepped toward her, then stopped again, glancing beyond her into the hall. "Is Lady Moorehead coming back down?"

"She said she'd join us in fifteen minutes." Mellie walked into the center of the room and sat down on a couch. "What is this about? You and I only just parted. I get the impression something urgent is at hand."

"No, no—nothing to be concerned about, anyway." He chose a chair across from her and seated himself, too. "I felt I needed to talk to you about the plate project."

She blinked. "What about it?"

"Well, hmm." He cleared his throat. "Where do I start? You are aware, of course, that I've been working hard to undo the damage caused by the second collapse in the trench. With the help of your groom, I've got the area in a decent state again.''

"Yes, you said as much in your last letter.''

He put his palms together and kneaded his hands nervously. "Leaving the project at this time was very frustrating for me. The plate is just sitting there, ready to come out.''

She gave a humorless laugh and looked away from him, leaning back in her seat. "Don't I know the feeling.''

Her demeanor had instantly grown cooler. The topic obviously reminded her why she'd been angry with him. He only hoped he could make up for his mistakes. "Yes. I mean, now I understand what you must have felt when your father ordered you to come to town. When I saw your expression upon hearing his announcement, I sympathized with you, but I didn't know how to oppose your father in front of everyone else. I wronged you then, and now I realize just how much.''

She held up a hand up and examined her nails. "That's all pretty much water under the bridge. I've been doing what I can to accept Papa's decision. I make good use of my time here . . . and, quite honestly, I've found that London does have its good points.''

Like handsome viscounts to flirt with? he thought with a frown. Or did she simply refer to the large variety of museums? Hoping for the latter, he said, "That's what Ben and I figured when we decided to come.''

Still not meeting his gaze, she got up and walked to a bay window at the front of the room. "I hope you enjoy your visit. Belzoni's exhibition may have turned out to be rather crass, but it was enjoyable, in its own way.''

He rose, too. "But not nearly as satisfying as working at our dig."

"Of course not!" She spun around and finally looked at him, her eyes narrowing. "Can't you see I'm trying to make the best of this situation? Is there a point to this discussion, Miles, or are you merely trying to remind me of all the reasons I have to be miserable?"

In a way, he was—but he'd do better showing her how *he* could make her happier. He moved toward her, until he stood only a few feet away. "I seem to be skirting my point. I came here to suggest that you return to Lowery Park with me as soon as possible. If you can be ready, we'll leave at dawn tomorrow."

Her jaw dropped, the aggravation on her face wiped away by shock. A moment passed before she regained her voice. "Is this some sort of joke?"

"I've never been more serious. You belong back at the dig site, completing your project. Surely whatever you've found to occupy you here can't be as important as that."

She sat back on the windowsill. "You don't know how much you tempt me. I do try to fit in here, but it's a constant struggle to keep myself tolerably distracted. Fortunately for me, Terry has so few friends left among the *ton* that the invitations we receive are limited. The thought of the first big ball we'll have to attend still fills me with dread."

"Then come home with me."

Her gaze shot to meet his. "But how could I explain my defection to Terry? And what about my father's wishes? Do you truly mean to defy him?"

He gave her a grim look. "I have no choice. Rest assured that I'll take responsibility for this. If I can't make Sir William see how much sense it makes for you to be at the Park now, I'll insist that he blame me, not you."

Another moment passed while she turned her head again and stared outside in silence. "Perhaps I could promise Terry I'll come back with Papa in a week, after you and I have extracted the plate."

His jaw tightened. If she was willing to make the journey to Dorset and back in one week, she must have a strong reason to return to London—the viscount, no doubt. But a week with her to himself was preferable to leaving her here with his rival. "That's a thought."

At last, she gave a small laugh. Looking back around at him, she said, "Very well. I'll go."

"You will?" The tension in his body melted. He nearly rushed up to embrace her but thought better of the impulse. The last thing he wanted was to scare her off just when he'd barely convinced her. Instead, he smiled. "Wonderful."

Getting up, she shook her head. "My sister is going to throw a fit."

"Do you want me to stay and help you try to explain?"

"No, that won't be necessary. I've been facing Terry's wrath all of my life. 'Tis nothing new to me. But what about Ben? Will he be willing to arrive at the Park with me in tow, in defiance of my father?"

He swallowed, hoping his next revelation didn't change her mind about going. "He's decided to stay here in London for a while longer—but not because he's worried about this. He agrees that I should take you home."

In fact it was his idea—but Miles didn't want to tell her that. Let her think that *he,* not Ben, had thought to reunite her with her work.

"So it's just you and me all the way to Dorset." She took a deep breath. "Clearly Terry won't want to leave London to chaperon me. I wonder if she'll consider the trip scandalous if I only bring my maid along."

When she voiced those words, the enormity of their plan hit Miles. If anything delayed them and they had to stop overnight, Mellie would be compromised and he obliged to marry her. He asked himself if that possibility deterred him. No. Though the idea of his marrying was new to him, the prospect wasn't nearly as frightening as the thought of her marrying *someone else.*

"I hope not," he said, still worried that Euterpe might thwart his plans.

"Well, then, I suppose we've got packing to do. You said we can leave at dawn?"

"Yes." He started toward the hall but stopped again. "If you have any remaining doubts, please tell me now, and I'll do whatever I can to reassure you."

She shook her head, meeting his gaze solidly. "I have no doubts. I'll be ready when you arrive tomorrow morning."

He smiled. She seemed determined to go. Now all he had to do was convince her he was the man for her, rather than the viscount. If anything would show her how compatible they were, then working together again had to do it.

As he went to the front door, he bit his lip. He only hoped compatibility would be enough to close the rift between them that his faltering had created.

Mellie saw Miles to the door and watched from the window until he drove away in the phaeton. She supposed she should have been leery about this scheme, given the risk it posed to her relationship with her family—and to her reputation. Instead she felt excited, relieved, thankful. She would be with Miles constantly for the next few days, traveling and then working. Half an hour ago, she'd feared she might not see him again while he was in London. He had acted so distant after Ben had caught them practically embracing earlier.

She closed her eyes, remembering the feel of his body against hers, the security of his arms wrapped around her. Reminded today of the wonder that touching him afforded, she hadn't known how she would bear four more weeks unable even to see him. This new development merely delayed the inevitable separation, but at the moment she cared only that she'd be with him again for the next week. She wouldn't think beyond that.

"Is Miles gone already?"

The sound of her sister's voice right behind her made her jump. She spun around. "Terry! I didn't hear you come downstairs. Yes, he left a few moments ago."

"That's too bad." Eyebrows drawing together, her sister looked closely at her. "Did he have anything *particular* to say?"

She nodded, turning back toward the drawing room to avoid scrutiny. "Come in here for a moment, and I'll tell you."

"Nothing is wrong, is it?" Terry asked, following her into the room.

"Well . . ." She paused until she had closed the doors behind them. Forcing herself to look her sister in the eye, she said, *"You* might not be totally pleased by the news—but I beg you to try to understand."

"To understand what? Miles said he only wanted to talk to you about your project."

"Yes, the plate project is part of this—but not all." She hugged herself nervously. "Forgive me. This isn't going to be easy for me to explain."

"Please, Mellie." Terry put her hands on her hips. "The suspense is likely worse than whatever you're hiding."

"Come, let's sit." She led her sister into the center

of the room, and they settled down on two chairs, facing each other. "Miles has offered to take me back to Lowery Park ... tomorrow. I'm afraid that I've accepted his invitation. I have to. After Miles and I have extracted the plate, I'll come back to London with Papa. If all goes as I expect, I'll only be gone a week— I promise."

For a moment, Terry merely studied her face. Then a faint smile tugged at the corners of her lips. "Very well. Do what you must. Just be careful."

Mellie's eyes widened with shock. "You're willing to let me miss a week of the Season?"

She shrugged. "My main reason for wanting you here for the Season was to heighten your chances of finding a good *parti,* but perhaps the man for you cannot be found in London."

A possible explanation for her sister's charity dawned on her. "Oh, you mean because Rodney has left town?"

Terry set her elbow on the arm of the chair and leaned her chin on her fist. "Do you think Rodney is the one for you?"

"No." She looked down into her lap, unnerved by her sister's probing gaze yet disarmed by her gentle response. "To be frank ... it's embarrassing for me to admit ... but I have a bit of *tendre* for Miles."

"I've been getting that impression."

"You have?" Mellie looked up at her and saw that she was grinning. Terry knew how she felt about Miles? Some of her tension relaxed. "Goodness, I wish I'd spoken to you about it before."

"Me, too, but I suppose you weren't ready."

"Oh, I'm not ready for anything." She stood and went to the fireplace, staring into the empty hearth. "What goes on in men's minds is a mystery to me."

Her sister got up and came to her side, putting a

hand on her shoulder. " 'Tis the same for all of us, dear. You've heard Shakespeare say, 'The course of true love never did run smooth.' "

"Perhaps that saying is true. I believe that Miles feels some attraction to me, but whenever he shows it, he backs away again. He truly must be a confirmed bachelor." She peered at Terry from the corners of her eyes. "Do you think there's any hope of his changing his mind?"

She smiled. "You've changed *your* mind about marriage, haven't you?"

Mellie hesitated for a moment, then nodded.

Her sister took a few steps away, then spun around with a flourish, one eyebrow raised. "Well, I've been planting a seed in Miles' head on your behalf. The other day when he first arrived in town, I let him know you were out with another man—and that you'd had two other engagements with the fellow in one week. I daresay Miles is convinced that you have another serious suitor. That's likely why he's decided to take you back to the Park now."

Mellie frowned, doubtful. "He said he asked me strictly for professional reasons."

"Oh, he *would.*" Terry waved her hand in a dismissive gesture. "He's probably testing the waters, still a bit hesitant to declare himself to you. It may take a while for him to shake off his 'confirmed bachelorhood' entirely. For now, I suggest that you let him continue to believe that Rodney might beat him to the punch."

"Do you think so?"

"Certainly. Nothing attracts a man to a woman more than seeing that other men are attracted to her. Don't overdo it, of course. You don't want him to think you and Rodney are betrothed, or anything quite so conclusive. Just make Miles aware that he has competition."

She thought about her sister's advice. Falling into Miles' arms today certainly hadn't helped her cause— nor had allowing him to kiss her the other week. If showing him her vulnerability only drove him away from her, then perhaps acting coy would prove a more successful tactic. She nodded slowly. "You just may have a point."

Terry giggled. "That's not a concession I often hear from you."

Despite her nervous state, Mellie smiled. "Perhaps I should listen to you more often. I know I've been hard on you for years but only because I've missed you so much. When you left Papa and me, I resented you for it. Looking back, I suppose I acted in a childish way."

"How could you not? You *were* a child." Terry rushed forward and gave her a hug. When they released each other again, her eyes looked watery. "Don't think it was easy for me to leave you, either. You and Father mean the world to me. Thank heavens Clio and her family soon followed Moorehead and me. Otherwise, I don't know how I would have lasted more than a few months."

A revelation struck Mellie. "You didn't want to go, did you? You only went because you loved Moorehead so much."

She let out a little laugh and pulled a handkerchief out of her pocket. Dabbing at her eyes, she said, "He wasn't the best prospect I had, but he put me so at ease. I can't explain why, but I never felt I had to try to impress him, the way I did with other men I'd tentatively set my sights on."

Memories flooded back to Mellie now—how her father had expressed open doubts about the man, especially about his ventures in Antigua. As for Mellie herself, she'd never disguised her resentment over her sisters' leaving the country. She had never understood it—yet now she, too, was defying her father's wishes, partly because she wanted to complete her project, but mostly because she longed to be near Miles. If Miles ever wanted her to live in Egypt with him, would *she* leave her family to do so?

She very likely would.

Guilt washed over her. She hadn't supported her sisters in their life choices, and they probably could have used any vote of confidence they could get. Moving to Antigua couldn't have been easy for Terry, who loved the social whirl here—and, naturally, loved her family.

"I behaved like the indulged child I was." Mellie put her hand up to her forehead. "Worse yet, I've continued thinking only of myself, though I'm hardly a child now."

"Growing up isn't as easy as it looks."

She shook her head. "I gave you no encouragement, yet here you are, encouraging me. If you had your choice, Miles wouldn't be the one you'd want me to marry. Obviously, you'd prefer Rodney."

Terry shrugged. "Being related to Gwyn would have been fun, but Miles is hardly a bad catch. I believe I may even have considered pursuing him myself at one time, but there was no spark between us. The two of you, on the other hand, have a world of interests in common. He'll make you happier than Rodney ever could."

Mellie's heart constricted with longing. "He *would* make me happy, I think."

Her sister placed a hand on her shoulder. "Don't fret unnecessarily, dear. How can Miles help but fall in love with someone as beautiful and intelligent as you? Now go and pack your things. Take everything, just in case you're not back in a week, after all.''

Mellie gave her a teary smile. ''I don't suppose you'd like to come along and chaperon me?''

She shook her head. ''It's only a day trip—and Miles is a friend of the family. I can't imagine him ever making any sort of improper advance on you.''

Now Mellie had her chance to confide the rest of her story, but she thought she'd rather not tempt her sister to change her mind. ''I'll take Peggy with me, of course.''

''Right. I'll find her now and send her to you to help pack.'' Terry started toward the back of the house.

''Thank you,'' Mellie called after her and turned toward the stairs. As she hurried to her bedchamber, her fears of losing Miles remained with her, but knowing that her sister supported her helped. Perhaps Terry didn't understand every aspect of her life, but she understood how important Miles was to her—and she cared. For the first time Mellie felt what an advantage her sister's move to York would be. Clio's family might well move back to England soon, too.

Miles might still leave her life at the end of the summer—but at least she wouldn't be left alone.

Fourteen

Miles guided the horses along the Dorset Road at a good fifteen miles an hour. As soon as the carriage had rolled through the city gates, he and Mellie had usurped the box from the coachman, relegating him to the back with his tiger. Meanwhile, Mellie's maid napped inside, allowing Miles to have her mistress all to himself.

With spirits as brisk as the horses' pace, he nodded to two laborers in a passing field. As the men pulled their forelocks in return, he said to his companion, "I still can hardly credit that your sister gave us her blessings to make this journey. When she came outside to see us off this morning, I expected her to renege at any moment."

She smiled. "Her support surprised me, too, but she and I had a wonderful little coze yesterday after you left. Despite my reluctance to come to London, I have to admit this visit has had some beneficial results. Terry and I have come to understand each other like never before."

"Do you have regrets about leaving her now?"

"I felt a twinge of guilt when we drove away this morning. She had tears in her eyes when she waved good-bye—but I keep telling myself that getting too emotional would be silly. I'll only be gone for a week."

He peeked at her profile. Could a week possibly be long enough to prove to her that she should marry him rather than the viscount? "Perhaps we can stretch out your time at home a bit longer than that. I know you've had trouble finding ways to entertain yourself in London."

"Actually, it hasn't been too bad." She glanced at him but didn't hold his gaze. "The main reason I've been restless is because I've been dying to reach the plate—if indeed it is a plate. Once we've recovered the piece and know what we have, I won't mind being away from the Park so much."

"Have you indeed enjoyed your, er, ventures in town?" He particularly wanted to know about her outings with his rival but felt hesitant to ask. How would he react if she gushed about the fellow's virtues?

"I have. Terry's shortage of acquaintances has kept her from carting me off to too many social engagements. Instead, I've had plenty of time to visit historical sights."

"With your maid?" he probed cautiously.

"Sometimes." She flicked an invisible speck from her sleeve. "Sometimes with a friend."

He clenched his fists. She had to be referring to the viscount. Learning more would help him size up the competition, but dread prevented him from asking outright. What if she revealed they had some sort of understanding? What if they were already betrothed?

For the next few miles, he danced around the subject until the suspense grew too unbearable for him. The sun had risen high in the sky when he finally resolved to steer the conversation in that direction again.

"Your sister says she's been impressed with your social graces." He felt the muscles in his jaw tense as he broached the subject. "She seems happy with your success in London."

Face turned away, she watched a family of ducks waddling beside the road. "I can't say I've had many real tests."

"From what Lady Moorehead says, you've taken London by storm with your charms."

"Oh, indeed." She laughed. "My many charms."

"Apparently, you've made *some* friends," he insisted. "You mentioned that someone has been accompanying you to historical sights."

She stared at the roadside for another moment. In a more sober voice, she said, "I've been fortunate enough to gain a new acquaintance who doesn't mind squiring me about. Terry's especially pleased about our . . . our association. Rodney is the brother of one of her old schoolmates."

Rodney. He stiffened, fixing his gaze straight ahead. "Yes, she told me you have a . . . a suitor you see frequently."

Again, her reply took an extra second or two. "Did she?"

Her tone was difficult to interpret, and when he glanced at her, she turned away. He suspected that her sister had betrayed a confidence. "Perhaps you feel the subject is none of my business. Do you not wish to speak about it?"

She shrugged, still not meeting his gaze. " 'Tis a strange subject for me to speak about—one to which I'm not accustomed. But I suppose if I must adapt to having a London debut, I shall have to be open to having suitors, as well."

The horses danced a little, and he realized he'd tightened his hold on the reins. He gave them more slack and cleared his throat. "How, er, helpful that you've had someone to escort you. You were worried you'd be bored during your Season. I gather that hasn't been a problem?"

"No, it hasn't." She opened her reticule and looked inside, fishing out a handkerchief. "Of course, I've missed Lowery Park—when it came to mind—but I've wasted little time with regret. Terry's frequent shopping excursions can still be tiresome, but, in between them, Rodney and I fit more appealing activities into my schedule."

He frowned. "Then his interests lie somewhat along the same lines as yours?"

"Oh, yes, they seem to." She dabbed at her pert nose and put away the lacy cloth again. "When I return to London, I expect he and I will visit the other historical sites and museums left on my list of things to see."

The assumption made him wince. He searched his brain for something to say to make himself look more to advantage and this Rodney person less so. Surely, the viscount must have little archaeological knowledge compared to *him*. "Have you told him much about your work?"

"Of course. You know I can't go long without speaking of that. Rodney's been exceedingly kind about listening to me. I imagine such prattle could be tedious for someone outside of the field."

"So he has no *natural* interest in archaeology?" He met her gaze, fighting to ward off a scowl.

She blinked at him. "I don't believe he thought much about the subject in the past, but since he and I met he's certainly warmed up to it. Just the other day, he was telling me how much he would love to visit the villa."

"Indeed." He looked back to the road, his bitterness

increasing moment by moment. "It sounds as though you two have become rather close. I'm surprised you'd leave London without saying good-bye to him."

"Rodney's out of town on business. I'll likely return before he does." After an instant, she added, "Your invitation couldn't have come at a more convenient time."

Now the scowl took over his face well and truly. She made it sound as though she'd left with *him* only because the viscount wasn't available to her. He drove in silence for several minutes, then decided he must keep learning about his rival if he had any hope of prevailing over him. "I believe you said this Rodney fellow is brother to one of Lady Moorehead's friends? Might I be acquainted with the family?"

She coughed, as though the question caught her off guard. Clapping one hand on her chest, she said, "You may. Do you recall ever meeting a, er, Lady Staughton?"

"Staughton? There's something familiar about—" Suddenly he placed the name and spun his head to face her. "Why, you can't mean Gwyneth Gough!"

She cringed. "Yes—but you mustn't think Rodney is like his sister. I'll be the first to admit that *she* is intolerable. Just because they're siblings doesn't mean they need be much alike. Only look at Terry and me."

"Good God. *Gough* is the one we've been talking about?" The heat of suppressed rage rose around his neck. He knew the viscount, and from all he'd seen the man was actually worse than his sister.

Yanking the horses to a stop in the middle of the road, he shifted on the box to face her. "That *coxcomb* has been squiring you about for two weeks?"

Her cheeks flushed. She glanced around at the servants watching them from the back of the carriage, then turned back to him with clenched teeth. "Resume driving, please."

He glared at her for a second, then threw a look back at the attendants. When they turned away, he took a deep breath and picked up the reins again.

As the horses proceeded, he grappled to regain his composure. "Pray forgive my outburst. I wish I could let the subject go without further comment, but I fear I cannot. I won't allow that knave to make a fool of you any longer."

She gasped. "How dare you suggest that I'm being made a fool by anyone? You know nothing of Lord Gough's intentions toward me. Not *every* man is a . . . a confirmed bachelor, Miles."

He closed his eyes, pain piercing through him. Forcing himself to look at her again, he croaked, "Has it come to that, then, Mellie? Are you and Gough betrothed?"

"I don't see that it's any of your business." She crossed her arms over her chest and turned her back to him.

Her declaration stung, as it implied he had no chance with her. "Perhaps not, but I'm still compelled to warn you: Gough will do you nothing but harm. From this point onward, you must cut him entirely."

She spun back around to face him. "Who are you to tell me what I must do? I have one father already, and he gives me quite enough edicts without your adding to them. Besides, as I told you, my sister knows Rodney, and she's happy to encourage my friendship with him."

"Your sister must not know him as well as she thinks." He kneaded his forehead, unsure where to start his explanation. Meeting her gaze, he said, "I fear I've made a mull of this, Mellie, but what I have to tell you is important. Unfortunately, it's also going to hurt you. Gough is a scoundrel—a renowned one. Lady Moorehead obviously doesn't know about the scandal. Likely she had already left for Antigua when the incident occurred."

Her brows drew together. "What incident?"

He faltered, still loath to bear bad tidings to her. "Has no one else in London advised you about Gough?"

"Advised us what? I told you we don't have many connections in town. Good heavens, Miles, please come out with whatever it is you're trying to say."

He nodded. "It's the only thing I can do. I wouldn't want to see your fortune go the way his has. To start with—rather abruptly, I'm afraid—Gough has been overfond of gaming from the time he and I were both at Oxford."

"A gamester." Her eyes narrowed. "Why, I never saw any sign of it—not that I have reason to doubt you. You say you've known him since your school days?"

"Yes, and I have more to tell you. When we were at university, he did relatively little harm other than waste his quarterly allowance. Then he reached his majority and came into much more money—more stakes, in his way of thinking. He set himself up in London and frequented not only the respectable men's clubs but some of the worst gaming hells in the city."

"And he lost a great deal of money?" she asked, her tone grown quiet. She looked away at the passing fields.

"Indeed he did. Were his family estate not entailed, he surely would have lost even the house. Then suddenly he seemed to stumble onto a winning streak. His luck continued for months. But one night after he'd torn through every club in London, raking in astounding winnings, he was caught exchanging a marked deck of cards for one of the house decks at White's."

She gasped, turning back to him with wide eyes. "He was cheating? Right in the midst of one of the most respected gentlemen's clubs in London?"

He nodded, his lip curling. "My uncle was there that night. He and the others present demanded that Gough return his ill-gotten gains and leave the country."

Her eyes glazed over in thought. "That must have been why he went to live in Geneva."

"No, he didn't leave England then. Since he'd sunk his winnings into other excesses, perhaps he had no money to start up a life on the Continent. A month after his exposure, one of his former victims—a friend of my uncle's—ran into him at a horse race outside of London. Gough was inviting unsuspecting onlookers to play cards at a private gaming hell. This time my uncle's mate challenged him to a duel. The event took place and Gough was injured. My uncle personally saw that Gough did his mending overseas."

"His hip injury . . . Oh, my God." She looked away, putting her hand over her mouth. "This . . . this is all too much. You must pardon me. I don't even know what to say."

"You do believe me then?"

"I only wish I had reason to question your story. The extent of his guilt is difficult to fathom. How can he continue to go about London as if none of this ever happened? How does he get away with it?"

"I can only speculate that he avoids the people most familiar with the scandal. My uncle's gone now, so Gough needn't worry about him. Perhaps his sister helps him determine where he can show his face. I doubt anyone truly respectable receives him—except, of course, those who aren't aware of his history, such as Lady Moorehead. Does he attend many parties?"

"None, I believe. He claims to feel uncomfortable

because he cannot dance. He told me about a . . . a hip injury he has.''

"A legacy from his duel." He studied her ashen face and felt even more sick. She had clearly cared about the fellow, perhaps even planned to marry him. "I can't tell you how dreadful I feel about telling you all of this, but if I hadn't, you might not have found out until you'd . . . until it was too late. Gough is charismatic and clever and knows nothing better than how to deceive. I hope this blow isn't too much for you."

She shook her head and covered her eyes with her hands, clearly overcome, though she tried to put on a brave face. "I shall recover. Please, let's not speak of it anymore. In fact, if you wouldn't mind, I'd rather not talk at all for a while. I fear I'm not quite up to conversation."

"That's understandable." His throat tight, he turned his attention to the road.

The rhythmic clopping of hooves on packed dirt provided an ironically soothing backdrop for poor Mellie's heartbreak. The situation was ironic for him, too, he realized. His rival had been ousted from competition sooner than he could have dreamed—but only in one sense. Perhaps there was no longer a question of Mellie's marrying the scoundrel, but she would undoubtedly continue to think of him for a long time to come.

In his mind he again saw the turmoil on her face when he'd told her the truth about Gough. Until that moment he'd had no idea how much his adversary had meant to her. Now he had to wonder when, if ever, she would be prepared to give her heart to a man again. First *he* had let her down with his vacillation, and now Gough with his unsavory dealings.

As the sun began to sink in the sky, they drove on

in silence. He could think of nothing to say to ease her pain, and she said nothing to him.

Mellie watched the daylight dwindle, feeling more stupid than she'd ever before felt. Her attempt at acting coy had backfired. Instead of looking like a sophisticated woman with a slew of suitors to choose from, she'd come across as a pathetic fool incapable of discerning whether a man was worthy of her esteem or not. She never should have tried feigning a finesse she didn't have. If Miles had had any shred of respect left for her after she'd fallen all over him, he'd surely lost the last of it now.

She stared off into the distance, unseeing in her humiliation.

After several miles, however, the dusky sky began to come alive with tinges of reds and purples. As the miles passed and the colors slowly deepened, she couldn't help but admire the beauty of the sunset, despite her state of despair.

"Extraordinary, is it not?" she asked Miles quietly.

He darted a surprised look at her.

She nodded toward the western horizon, then sat gazing at it for another moment, a faint smile pulling at her lips. When she turned back to him, he was watching her. She didn't know if he had even looked at the sky.

"I've never seen anything more lovely," he said, his expression sober.

A misguided wish that he referred to *her* flooded her head. She looked away again quickly. "Perhaps everything is lovelier when one is returning home."

"If that's the case, then Lowery Park must be very much like home to me."

Obviously he was trying to show her some warmth

out of compassion, and his kindness told her that he felt some concern for her. At least he didn't despise her for her foolishness. Gratitude welled up inside her. "I'm pleased that you've come to feel that way."

"I'm pleased that you're pleased," he said.

Now he was doing it a little too brown. She went back to watching the sun fade away.

When the carriage finally came to a stop before the front of Lowery Manor, twilight had fallen. The coachman strode around from the back and took the reins to hold the horses.

Miles stood up on the box, stretching his arms. "Here at last."

By the time she'd gathered up her reticule and put on her gloves, he had jumped to the ground. When she slid across the bench to follow him, he held out both hands to her. She took hold of his shoulders, longing for the feel of his arms around her—but he only took her by the waist and eased her to the ground. She slipped from his grasp slowly, reluctantly.

"I'd best accompany you inside," he said as she stepped back and smoothed down her dress. "Your father will expect an accounting for your arrival."

She looked up at the big stone house and tried to imagine her father's reception. Would he be furious at them? She had no way of speculating, since she had never before defied him. She had never had a reason to do so.

Turning back to Miles, she said, "Now that we're here, it doesn't seem fair that you should have to face Papa's anger. I never should have agreed to let you bring me home. Go on to the gatehouse, and I'll tell him that I coaxed you into this scheme. He can't fault you for falling prey to my arts of persuasion. Until recently, *he* always gave in to my whims."

He shook his head. *"I'm* the one who persuaded *you,* and that's what I'm going to tell Sir William."

Before she could protest further, he started up the front steps. She wavered, then followed quickly. If she couldn't take all the blame for this, she wanted to make sure she took her share.

"Papa?" she called tentatively as they entered the main hall. She hurried past Miles and walked up to the study, tapping on the closed door. "Papa? It's me, Mellie. I've stopped home unexpectedly."

"Mellie?" his muffled voice penetrated the wooden panels. A chair scraped across the floor, succeeded by rapid footsteps. The door swung inward, and her father stood before her, a deep furrow in his brow. "Mellie, what are you doing home? Is something wrong?"

"Everything's fine, Papa, I assure you." She moved forward, obliging him to step back and allow her in the room.

Only then did he notice her companion. "Miles? Did you bring Mellie home? What's going on?"

" 'Tis nothing to worry about, sir," Miles said, his solemn tone making his words sound unconvincing. He entered the study as well. "I'll explain everything."

Once he'd cleared the threshold, Mellie closed the door and turned back to her father. "Pray forgive me, Papa, but this is all a whim of mine. I felt I had to come home and complete my project. Three more weeks was simply too long for me to wait."

"No, this was *my* idea, sir." Miles stepped in front of her. "I felt that for Mellie to be happy she needed to get back to her work. I coaxed her into leaving London. The blame lies entirely with me."

"It lies with me," Mellie insisted from behind him. *"I'm* the one who defied your orders, Papa. I know I shouldn't have done so, but I intend to be here only a week—maybe even less time than that. As soon as you're ready to visit London, I'll go back with you.''

Still frowning, the man looked back and forth between the two of them. ''Where's Euterpe?''

''Still in town,'' Mellie said. ''She gave us her blessings to make this journey, believe it or not.''

''Euterpe agreed to this?'' Her father shook his head to himself, then turned to Miles. ''And you went along with the plan as well? This whole situation confounds me. You were the one who helped persuade me that Mellie couldn't afford to miss any of her Season.''

Mellie frowned in confusion. She shot a look at Miles, expecting him to share her consternation.

''That was a mistake on my part,'' he said to her father, not meeting her gaze. ''I know you want what's best for your daughter, but what you want isn't to be found in London—at least, I hope not.''

Her father's eyes narrowed, but before he could respond Mellie stepped between the two men, facing Miles. ''What does Papa mean—*you* helped convince him?''

He looked down at her, his mouth a grim line. ''I'll explain that, too, after I've finished speaking with your father.''

''No. There can be no explanation.'' She stared at him, attempting to absorb the shocking truth. Miles had advised her father to send her to London early! He had wanted to be rid of her. Evidently he'd found her company irksome and wanted to work on her project alone. Why, then, had he kissed her—for sport? To puff her up, so she wouldn't suspect he wanted her gone? She couldn't fathom his motives, but one thing was clear: He had played her for a fool. She swallowed and said softly, ''I can't believe your duplicity.''

''Mellie, please,'' he said, his eyebrows tilted upward, "we'll discuss this in a moment. Right now, your father deserves a full explanation."

"And I don't?" She paced away from him, then spun back around. "You've been playing games with me—telling me one thing, doing another. For goodness' sake, you *kissed* me the night of my farewell dinner, after you'd advised my father to send me away!"

His glance at Sir William drew her gaze in the same direction. Her father lifted an eyebrow, his expression stern and alert. But, to her surprise, he remained silent.

She looked back at Miles, not caring that she'd revealed the secret. Her father had a right to know what his trusted guest did under his roof.

Miles faced her, his gaze unflinching. "That kiss was as unplanned as it was unforgivable. When I'd talked to Sir William I had no intention of—"

"Save your explanation for *him*," she interrupted, brushing past his shoulder on her way to the door. At the threshold, she looked to her father one last time. "At least now you know, Papa, what his guidance is worth. Perhaps you'll reconsider taking his counsel in the future."

Without waiting for a reaction she fled the room, darting through the hall to the rear of the house. She ran outside into the darkness and turned down a path that led to the villa. A line of trees to one side of the trail cast her in shadows, but she knew the route by heart. She needed to get away—away from everything but her work.

Let Miles explain himself to Papa now, she thought as she leapt over a large root that she remembered, rather than saw, in her path. She hoped the discussion the men were having upset them as much as they'd distressed her over the past few weeks. The two of them deserved one another! With any luck, they'd spend the evening locked up together in battle.

Then she would be left to herself . . . in peace.

What she would do the following day was another question. Perhaps she could catch the post chaise back to London. That would take her away temporarily from the men who had made her life miserable. But where would she go after the Season? Where could she continue to pursue her archaeological endeavors? With whom? As a woman, she wasn't likely to be taken seriously by many in the field.

Breathing hard, she slowed her pace to a walk as she approached the ruins. She passed the area where the mosaic lay and thought of Bennie. Perhaps he would have suggestions. When she returned to town tomorrow night, she would talk to him. In a man's world her chances weren't good, but she had her mind and her experience to speak for her—two assets that neither Miles nor her father could take away. She refused to dwell on what they *had* taken away. Instead, she would throw herself into her work and forget about men.

Swallowing hard against a growing lump in her throat, she turned toward the area where her plate lay.

Fifteen

Mellie skirted the east wall of the villa and walked up to the edge of the trench. Peering down into it, she could barely make out the silhouettes of rubble and equipment below her feet. Darkness blanketed whatever lay in deeper areas of the excavation. Coming here without a lantern had been foolish—and the idea of returning to the manor repulsed her.

Stooping to get a closer look, she discerned a clear spot on the floor of the trench. She leaned back on one hand and jumped down inside.

She took a moment to survey her surroundings as best as she could. When she'd last seen the area, the site had been filled with debris. Now much of the loose stone and soil had been cleared, but a few piles still remained.

Stepping around a heap of gravel in the center of the trench, she frowned. When she'd worked with Miles she had never known him to leave haphazard mounds of waste underfoot. He had certainly grown sloppy after she'd left.

She put her hands on her hips, disappointed in him

yet again. Perhaps until now she had only seen in him what she'd wanted to see—a dedicated archaeologist, a handsome face, a man attracted to her. Was nothing she had believed about him true?

"Mellie!" a male voice called in the distance.

Miles. A knot coiled in her stomach. Somehow he had slipped away from Papa already. She didn't want to face him, not now or ever. Ducking down, she held herself still.

"Mellie, are you out here?" her father's voice called, closer in distance than Miles' had been.

So, both of them had run out here after her. The show of solidarity when she had expected them to be at war vexed her. Well, if they weren't fighting with each other, she hoped they were racked with worry. She heard rustling on the nearby path and held her breath.

A faint yellow light arose on the east wall. As the source neared the trench, the area brightened. Then directly above her Miles appeared in the halo of a lantern. His eyes widened when he spotted her. "Mellie! Are you injured?"

She looked away from him, standing as her father arrived with a second lantern. "Of course not. Why would I be injured?"

"Because you ran all the way out here with no light to guide you," Sir William broke in, his voice stern. "You gave us one hell of a scare."

Pursing her lips, she didn't bother to answer. She turned to view the scene again now that the men had illuminated the trench. To her surprise, she found that several large holes gouged the soil near the plate.

"What happened here?" She stepped closer and saw that the digging had been done with harsh strokes of a shovel rather than the careful nibbles of an archaeologist's trowel. Pain squeezed through her chest. She spun around toward Miles. "What on earth did you think you were doing here? Turning over topsoil for a garden?"

"What do you mean?" Eyebrows drawing together, he scampered down into the hole.

She turned back around toward the torn ground, her face growing hot with rage. "I can't believe I trusted you with my project. You're a menace! Who knows what artifacts you may have damaged here?"

"None of this rubble was here when I checked the site the other morning," he said, his eyes wide. He set the lantern down and moved up next to her. "Before I left I sifted and cleared all of the loose bits. I don't understand. Sir William, have you been working here?"

"My father doesn't do work like *this*," Mellie spat at him. She grabbed the lantern and stepped around him, squatting down. Holding the light out in front of her, she got her first good view of the excavation and, with it, the full truth. The shovel gouges went deep into the earth—and nothing but soil was visible within them.

The plate was gone.

She collapsed down in the dirt on her bottom.

"What's wrong, Mellie?" Sir William asked. He shuffled down the side of the trench.

For a moment she couldn't even speak. Thoughts tore through her mind. What had happened? Only one possibility occurred to her. She stared at Miles until she drew his gaze. "I can't believe it—you stole the plate."

"That's absurd," her father said, stepping up beside them. "It's still buried here."

Miles shook his head, staring at the holes. "It does appear to be gone."

She snorted. "*Appear* to be? As if you don't know exactly where it is. Now I see everything as clear as day. You wanted me in London so you could continue my project by yourself and take the plate. Tell us where it is, Miles. You'll never get away with claiming you found it. If at any time in the future you suddenly reveal your discovery of a rare silver Roman plate to the archaeological world, my father, Ben, and I can all attest that you wrongly obtained it.''

He gaped at her. ''You think *I* would steal from you and your father? Lord, the impression I've made on you is even worse than I'd believed.''

Hoisting herself to her feet again, she lifted her chin to look him in the eye. ''Just give me back my plate. I don't care about anything else.''

''Miles didn't take it,'' her father said, examining the scene with a bleak face. ''I checked this area earlier today before I went back to the manor for tea. Everything at the villa was in order then. These holes were dug within the last couple of hours—while Miles was with you.''

She gulped. The situation was even more dreadful than she had thought. She'd wrongly accused Miles—though after all he'd done to her, she didn't much care. The worst thing was that the plate was truly gone, carried off by an unknown thief. So much for throwing herself into her work to forget about men. She had come within a hair's breadth of what might have been the most magnificent find of her life, and now she would never even glimpse it.

Miles turned to her. In a soft voice, he said, ''Mellie, I don't know what to say. This is so unfair, especially on top of everything I've already burdened you with today. This is all my fault. You entrusted me to take over your project during your visit to London. If only I'd stayed here, the plate never would have been stolen.''

''Don't be daft,'' she said without meeting his gaze.

"You've wronged me quite enough, but this had nothing to do with you."

Her father paced to the other end of the trench, rubbing his chin. "This is the first security problem we've ever had at the villa. The most precaution we've ever taken is posting a footman to watch over the entire Park at night."

"The thief can't have gone far in two hours." Miles looked out at the darkened fields around the pit. "Could it have been one of the servants at the manor?"

Sir William shook his head. "All of our staff have served us for years. I can't imagine finding the thief in that quarter."

"But who else would have been aware there was potentially a find of value here?" he asked. "I've told no one the kinds of details about this dig that would be necessary to reach the plate so easily."

A horrible thought made Mellie's eyes go wide. She wouldn't have believed she could feel worse than she had only a moment ago . . . but now she did.

"*I* have," she said in a small voice.

Both men swung around to face her.

She nodded and set down the lantern before it slipped from her shaking hand. "No wonder Rodney was so interested in my research. Remember, Miles? I told you he asked all about the villa—and he had to leave London suddenly this week when he found out my colleagues would be visiting me in town. How could I be so stupid?"

To her astonishment, he grinned. "But, Mellie, don't you realize what this means? If Gough is our man, we have a lead to follow. He can't be far ahead of us. Let's go and get him."

She looked up at his face and felt rather awed at the determination she read in his eyes. "But how can we possibly follow him? How would we know where he's gone?''

"The way I see it, Gough Lodge is a good place to start.''

"Does he still own it? Oh, yes. You said it was entailed.'' She took a deep breath and felt some of the strength return to her body.

"I'll go with you,'' Sir William said.

Miles frowned. "It might be best if you lead a search here, just in case he's still on the premises. Meanwhile, I'll go to Gough Lodge.''

"Do you think he's dangerous?'' Mellie asked.

He shook his head. "And he's not expecting trouble from anyone. Confronting him is easily a one-man job. Whether your father or I find him, we'll have the advantage of taking him by surprise.''

"Right.'' Picking herself up, she set her jaw. "He's most likely at Gough Lodge, I think. I'm going with you, Miles. He's not going to get away with this.''

Miles twisted his mouth and looked at Sir William.

Her father shook his head and turned to her. "Wait up at the house. Hunting down a thief is no office for a woman.''

"Oh, no.'' She puffed up her chest. "Don't try telling me you men will take care of everything. That claim doesn't impress me anymore. Miles doesn't know the best route from here to the Gough estate, but I sometimes rode there with Terry when she used to visit Gwyneth. I can get there through the woods in twenty minutes. From the road, it will take twice that time.''

Sir William frowned. "Can't you give Miles directions?''

"And risk his getting lost—now, when we won't get a second chance?'' She started climbing out of the trench. "Hardly. That plate is my find, and I'm getting it back.''

"Take her," her father said to Miles. "I know you'll do everything in your power to keep her safe. I'll send a servant out for a constable and have them meet you at Gough Lodge as soon as possible."

"I'll meet you at the stables," Mellie called back to Miles, already running back toward the house.

He caught up with her within a minute, and they jogged to the stables without speaking. By the time they'd thrown saddles on two horses, a footman had arrived with instructions to seek a constable. As they rode out of the yard, two other servants came out of the house to search the grounds with Sir William.

"We'll need to stop at the gatehouse and fetch my pistols," Miles called to her over the sounds of the horses.

"Pistols?" She threw a shocked look at him.

"I don't expect to use them, but bringing them might be a good precaution."

She hesitated, then nodded. "I daresay you're right." Spurring on her horse, she led the way to the gatehouse.

Miles stopped there for less than five minutes, then they continued through the woods toward the Gough estate. Mellie's thoughts moved as quickly as her horse galloped. What if Rodney wasn't there when they arrived? If he got away, she swore she'd squeeze information about his whereabouts out of his worthless sister. She would get her plate back, come hell or high water.

They emerged from the darkness of the woods into an overgrown park dimly lit by a newly arisen moon.

"There's the house," she said, pointing at a large square silhouette along the western horizon.

Both riders gave their reins a tug, and the horses slowed.

"There are no lights on at all." Her shoulders went limp. "It appears we've come up short."

"Not necessarily," Miles said. "Judging by the sorry state of this park, the Lodge is uninhabited. If Gough is here alone, he'll hardly light up the entire place. In fact, we may have a difficult time finding him before he spots us. I suggest we make the rest of our approach on foot."

"Good idea." She halted her mare and slipped down to the ground.

Miles joined her on the neglected lawn. "With so many trees and bushes, we should have no trouble finding an inconspicuous spot to leave the horses."

They led the animals up a slight incline. As their view of the building grew more distinct, telltale signs of disrepair became apparent. What had once been a handsome home now boasted boarded-up windows, crumbling eaves, and riotously climbing vines of ivy.

The soft neighing of a horse in the distance stopped them in their tracks.

Miles shot a look toward a cluster of outbuildings where the noise had originated. "Well, the stables aren't empty, so it seems *someone* is here. We'd better take the horses around to the far side of the house before they decide to strike up a conversation with their counterpart."

"I'm right behind you."

He looked at her and frowned. "Wait. I think it would be safer if you return to the woods while I go on. I must have had windmills in my head to agree for you to come this far."

She met his gaze squarely. "If the situation is dangerous, I can't allow you to walk into it alone. This theft is my fault, remember. I insist on helping you."

"I can handle Gough on my own. From what I know of him, he's not dangerous, only deceitful."

"Then you can have no objection to my coming with you." When she saw him still hesitate, she added,

''Frankly, I'd be more afraid left alone in the woods than if I continued with you.''

He frowned. ''Maybe we should wait for the constable to arrive. We can watch the house until then.''

''And what if Rodney notices us and escapes through the back? I don't want to risk his getting away. I have far too much at stake.''

He squinted up at the dark building and sighed. ''Well, if he's here, chances are he's alone. Let's move closer—but I reserve the option of changing my mind if the situation begins to look dangerous.''

She nodded and they walked on with the horses until they reached the opposite side of the park. Finding a tall, partially collapsed fence, they secured the animals to two posts that still held solid.

''Let's walk along the front of the house first,'' she said, scanning the area. ''It looks in better shape than the back.''

He nodded. Dipping in the pocket of his jacket, he pulled out a pistol and held the handle out to her with the nose down. ''Take this.''

Swallowing down her fear, she accepted the gun. The metal handle felt cold and heavy.

He took out a companion pistol for himself. ''Please be *extremely* careful, Mellie. That gun is loaded, though the safety latch is on. Do you know how to trip it if need be?''

She shuddered and gave a nod, gingerly positioning the firearm in her hand. ''My father has taught me how to shoot, and the gun he used to show me was much like this.''

''Let's hope your lessons won't be put to the test tonight.'' Gesturing for her to follow, he started around the building. They crept past a dozen boarded-up windows and an occasional gaping hole fringed with sharp glass teeth.

As they turned the second corner, a metallic clatter rang out inside the house, and they both started. It sounded as though someone had dropped a cooking pot.

"I vow," Mellie hissed, "if he just dropped my fifteen-hundred-year-old Roman plate, I will kill him."

"Please try not to pursue that line of thought while you have that pistol in your hand," Miles whispered. "The noise might have been anything. Judging by all the chimneys overhead, we're near the kitchen. That clattering may only have been a pot falling in the scullery. Stand guard here, and I'll have a look inside."

"I will not." She drew back her shoulders. "You'll need *me* to show you the way to the scullery."

He moved up close to the house and peered in a broken window. "If only one of us enters, it halves the chances of our knocking something over and being discovered."

She glided up beside him. "Then I should be the one to go in. Being smaller and more familiar with the house, I'm less likely to stumble and be caught."

"What if there are rats? One squeal, and we're finished, you know."

"I presume you mean a squeal from the rat and not me," she said, lifting her chin.

He looked at her long and hard, but she met his gaze the entire time, showing no sign of fear . . . she hoped.

Finally, he turned back to their point of entry. "I see there's no use trying to talk sense with you. We'll both go in, but I want you to stay well behind me. If we see someone, please remain hidden and allow me to approach. In the case of possible danger, don't reveal yourself. Keep quiet and wait for a chance to escape later."

"Understood." She gripped her pistol tightly, pointing its nose at the ground.

"Fine. We'll enter here and make our way around to the kitchen. By the time we approach the scullery, our eyes should be accustomed to the dark. Is there a main corridor running east-west along this side of the building?"

She nodded. "The kitchen is at the end. I imagine the scullery is through there."

"A safe assumption, I should think." He tugged at the decayed frame of the window, and it broke off in his hand, leaving a huge hole in the wall. "Even *I* will have no trouble squeezing through here. The only possible danger is from jagged edges that could cut us or snag our clothing."

She gave a nervous giggle. "Perhaps I should have worn my digging breeches tonight."

He snorted. "I think we're better off without every contour of your legs delineated and distracting me. Now, from this point on, we must be virtually silent."

Did her legs truly distract him? she wondered, despite the seriousness of the situation.

He clambered through the casement and dropped into the house soundlessly, then turned and reached back to help her.

Holding his arm with one hand and the pistol with the other, she stepped inside with ease. Reluctantly, she let go of him and paused to let her eyes adjust. They'd landed in the library, though nearly all of its shelves stood bare. In place of the ornate furniture that had once graced the room stood only a decrepit desk, a rickety table, and three mismatched chairs. A few volumes and papers lay strewn over the wooden floor, completely devoid of carpeting.

Directing her attention to Miles, she found him watching her. She gave him a nod to continue.

He inched toward the doors to the hall, holding a hand out behind him in warning.

"Stay back," he whispered.

Fortunately for her nerves, the doors stood open wide, so she had no need to worry whether they would creak or what might lay beyond. In another stroke of luck, the thick carpeting in the corridor remained intact to muffle their footsteps. She and Miles advanced without a sound.

He motioned again for her to wait, and she gave him a belligerent nod. Standing with her arms crossed over her chest, she watched him edge up the hall. The further he progressed, the more aware she became of the darkness and the isolation. For the first time, she noticed that the evening had grown chilly. She drew her arms tighter against her body.

When her companion had nearly vanished in blackness, she began to tiptoe up the hall in his wake. Keeping her eyes fixed on his dark form, she used her free hand to feel her way along the tattered and dusty wallpaper.

At one dreadful moment she tripped on a crumpled tarp and nearly tumbled headfirst. In the nick of time she caught the molding of a nearby door and regained her balance. Gasping for breath, she looked up the hall and saw that Miles hadn't noticed. She thanked her lucky stars. Had she fallen, she would have given them away.

While she watched, he vanished through the doorway to the kitchen. Mindful of her footing, she crept forward faster and reached the door seconds after him. She peeked in, astonished to find the far end of the room illuminated by a light seeping through from the scullery. Miles stood in the glow, unflinching and glaring into the other room. She noted that he held no weapon.

Only then did she realize she had no idea what he planned to do next. Over the pounding of her heart, she distinguished tinkering noises coming from the scullery.

"Polishing things up for a dinner party, Gough?" Miles asked. He stepped through the doorway and out of her view. "One can only imagine the kind of entertaining you must do with your connections and such a house."

A loud metallic clattering from the region indicated that Rodney had been startled into dropping something. Her plate? She gritted her teeth and stole across the room, clutching her pistol.

"Kennestone," she heard Rodney say, his tone a mixture of fear and indignation. "Or St. Leger now, isn't it? What in God's name are you doing here?"

"I'm here because I have reason to believe that you, as usual, are in possession of something that doesn't belong to you. I intend to restore that article to its rightful owner."

"If you're looking to recoup any of your uncle's gambling losses, I fear I shall have to disappoint you." A hint of faltering marred the defiance in Rodney's voice. "I don't have a damn shilling to my name. I should think that would be obvious, given the state of my home."

"Indeed. But what is that you're holding?"

Unable to resist looking, Mellie peeked around the molding and saw Rodney lift a large, blackened platter from a work table. *Her* plate! A bucket of polish and a pile of rags lay on the table, and part of the plate's coating had been scrubbed off to reveal a shining core. There could be no further doubt of the artifact's silver composition.

"This?" he asked. The flickering light of a small fire in the hearth revealed the shine of perspiration on his brow. "This is merely an old platter I uncovered in the cellars. I'm trying to ascertain if it might have any value.''

''Such a plate was left to lie around in the cellars? I find that odd, since there seems to be little else left in this house. How do you suppose a piece like that escaped notice until now?''

Rodney shrugged. ''Quite a few things remain in the cellars. This plate was there for anyone to take.''

Miles' veiled expression turn into a scowl. ''The local constable may not see it that way when Miss Lowery tells him her side of the story.''

The blood drained from the thief's face. For a split second she thought he would faint. Before she realized what was happening, he recovered and lifted the bulky artifact above his head, preparing to heave it toward his accuser.

''No!'' she screamed. She sprang out of her crouch and pointed her pistol at him. Frightened for Miles' life and enraged by such abuse of the plate, she summoned the fury it took to pull the trigger. She didn't want to kill him, but she wanted him hurt, so she aimed for his shoulder.

An explosion sounded . . . then all went black.

Sixteen

"Mellie, can you hear me?" a familiar voice asked, seeping into her consciousness.

All was dark, and dizziness clouded her mind. She lay on a cold, hard surface, but someone held her head—someone with large, warm hands. Blinking open her eyes, she saw Miles looking down at her, a crease between his eyebrows.

"Where are we?" she murmured.

"You're awake." His shoulders relaxed visibly. "Are you injured?"

She shook her head, unaware of any pain. The dizziness began to clear. She noticed she lay beside a crude wooden table. Then her memory flooded back, and anxiety washed through her.

Rodney—she had shot him.

She tried to prop herself up on her elbows, darting looks about the scullery. To her astonishment, several other people had arrived on the scene. How long had she been out?

"Don't move, love," her father said, standing behind Miles. "Just lie back and rest."

She strained her neck to try to see Rodney across the room, but the local constable and one of her father's footmen blocked her view. A leather-encased leg stretched out past them on the floor, telling her that her victim lay sprawled.

Gulping, she looked back to Miles. "Is he . . . Did I . . ."

"Gough?" He glanced over his shoulder at the thief, then turned back to her. "I don't know whether the news will disappoint you or relieve you, but you missed him entirely. Your shot did, however, nudge a stew pot off a shelf above him. He took a pretty good blow on the head. He's out cold."

"Thank God." She let her head and shoulders drop back into his arms.

"How do you feel?" her father asked.

She directed her thoughts back to herself and grimaced in disgust. Had she truly succumbed to a fit of vapors? "I'm fine. Let me sit."

Using her arms for support, she eased herself into an upright position. The last vestiges of dizziness cleared, and she lifted a hand to push a lock of hair out of her eyes. "I can't believe I swooned. Such a *missish* reaction! Pray swear that neither of you will tell anyone about this."

The lines of concern on Miles' face softened. "I won't if you won't, since the story does *me* little credit. Not only did I lead a woman into peril, I ended up being rescued by *her*."

He still crouched beside her, his knee nearly touching her arm. Disconcerted by his proximity, she looked away from him. "Where's the plate? Is it damaged?"

"I caught it before it could hit the floor." He stood and retrieved the artifact from the table. In silence, he handed her the piece.

"Thank you," she managed to utter, a lump rising

in her throat. She took the plate carefully in both hands, supporting the bulk of the weight in her lap. Fingering the small area Rodney had polished, she studied the exposed handiwork. The relief was exquisite. A quick inspection of the rest of the surface revealed no major flaws.

"It's even more magnificent that I dreamed," she whispered. "If only I'd been present to see it uncovered."

"You ought to have been," her father said, his voice tight. "I wish I'd never sent you to London."

Looking up at him, she read a world of love and pain in his eyes. In that instant, she knew that everything he'd done had been for her sake—even sending her away from her work and himself. She waved off his statement. "No one could have foreseen this would happen."

"If it's any consolation, I believe there may be even more to the find." Miles grabbed a bulky canvas bag from the table and set it down on the floor beside her. "Gough seems to have some other plunder here. Why don't you check and see?"

Heart thumping in her chest, she gave the plate back to Miles. Surely there couldn't be a companion piece. She spread the opening of the sack so the three of them could glimpse the contents. Inside lay several smaller plates and a large pitcher, encrusted in the same manner as the original piece—and all apparently silver.

"Good heavens." She looked up at Miles and saw her own amazement reflected in his eyes. Then, a moan emitted from the other side of the table made them both start.

"Don't . . . don't kill me, Mellie," Rodney croaked out, still out of her view. "Please. I only took the pieces out of desperation—not malice. Honest."

She snorted, pulling the top of the canvas sack to

her chest. *"Honest?* You don't know the meaning of the word."

Miles sidestepped the other men to tower over the thief. "Don't address Miss Lowery again, Gough. If anyone is going to kill you now, it will be me—and I promise you *I* won't miss."

The constable held up a hand. "Please, my lord, stand aside. His fate is in the hands of the law now. Neither you nor Miss Lowery need ever trouble yourselves over him again."

Sir William walked to their side of the room. "May we take the stolen artifacts back to the Park tonight, Constable?"

"Aye." He moved to one side, giving Mellie her first look at the ropes binding Rodney's arms. "Gough just admitted taking them. We all heard the confession. 'Tis obvious where he got the goods. There's only one ancient Roman excavation in this neighborhood."

Sir William turned to Mellie. "You can take the pieces back to the dig site and examine them there, as you rightfully should have done when they were first uncovered."

A warmth filled her, despite the chill of the floor beneath her. Her father *did* understand what her work meant to her. After this incident he wasn't likely to come between her and a project again. She smiled at him and hauled herself up on wobbly legs. At least, not every aspect of her life lay in ruin. "Thank you, Papa."

Miles looked to the constable. "What will happen to Gough?"

The man surveyed his prisoner, his lip curling. "By rights, he ought to hang, but his rank will likely save his life. Fortunately for us, he has severed all lofty connections he once had. A sentence of transportation ought to stick."

Rodney struggled to sit up, meeting Mellie's gaze for the first time since she'd aimed a pistol at him. "Mellie, I never meant—"

"Don't speak to her." Miles cut him off. "She knows exactly what you meant in all your dealings with her."

The prisoner hung his head. "It wasn't all as you believe. Mellie truly is a charming woman. I've never met a more—"

"Spare me," she said, putting her hands over her ears. She couldn't bear looking at the man; it reminded her of her stupidity in befriending him. Grabbing a large polishing cloth from the table, she turned to Miles. "Let me wrap the plate in this. Can you get the other artifacts?"

"My pleasure." He handed her the plate and stooped to reclose the canvas sack. While at the floor, he reached under the table and pulled out the gun she'd used, securing the safety latch and stashing it in his pocket.

She swallowed and looked away.

Her father, she noticed, didn't seem to be preparing to go. Did he expect her and Miles to ride back to the Park alone? Now that her anxiety about the theft had passed, she remembered how Miles had betrayed her. Being alone with the man didn't appeal to her. "Are you coming with us, Papa?"

He shook his head. "I've had no hand in your project. You two worked hard on it, and you deserve time to savor the fruits of your labor privately. When you're ready to bring the goods up to the manor, I'll look at them there."

"At least ride back to the Park with us," she said.

"I'll accompany the constable back to the gaol, so he can take a statement from me."

The set of his jaw told her he wouldn't be swayed.

She supposed he felt a duty to ensure personally that Gough was put behind bars.

"Very well." She found a second, smaller canvas bag and stowed the plate in it. "Let's be off, Miles."

Pausing briefly to thank the constable and the footman, she got out of the scullery as quickly as possible. With Miles just behind her, she hurried through the dark halls, her bulky burden growing heavier with each step. She had to switch arms several times. When they finally reached the library, she climbed out the window and sat down on the grass outside, panting.

Miles stepped through the casement and squatted beside her. "You're in no condition to ride. I'm not about to have you faint again on the way home."

"Faint?" She balked at the word but couldn't think of an argument to make against his using it. "I'll be fine once we're on our way. All this excitement has merely overset me a bit."

He shook his head and stood. "Your mare will sense the stress and become upset. If you were to ride with me, do you think we'd have any trouble leading her?"

"Anima would follow us with no problem, but the precaution is hardly necessary. I'm perfectly all right." To try to prove her case, she struggled to her feet. Her knees buckled, and she nearly fell.

"I'd like you to ride with me anyway." He studied her face. "Please. Don't let your personal feelings stand in the way of your safety."

Truth be told, her personal feelings were mixed. Despite her anger with him—and disgust with herself—she secretly relished the chance to feel the warmth of his body against hers one last time. She'd been a bit hard on him tonight, too, and that didn't help her resolve. Ashamed of all of her weaknesses, she nodded and leaned over to pick up the bag containing the plate.

"Let me get that." He took both sacks, and they walked toward the horses' hiding place. "Shall we go straight to the villa, or would you rather stop at the manor and rest first?"

"The villa, of course. I'm not entirely a milksop, you know." She threw him an irritated look. "Let's try to reconstruct this event somewhat along the lines of how it should have unfolded."

He gave a humorless laugh. "If only we could do that with the past few weeks."

She stopped and bent over, pretending to tighten her bootlace, so he couldn't see her lip quivering. "I'm not sure we share an opinion on what should have been."

He continued toward the horses without responding, obviously unable to argue that he wanted the same thing she did.

After strapping their treasures onto Anima's back, he mounted the stallion he'd ridden to the estate. He looked to Mellie and held out a hand. "Come here."

She stepped up beside him but hesitated to take his hand. Before she knew what he was about, he leaned over and grabbed her under the arms. Lifting her like a doll, he positioned her sidesaddle in front of him. The warmth of his legs encompassed her left thigh and bottom. Her mind reeled. The position was almost unbearably intimate.

"I fear I shall have to hold you." He wrapped an arm around her midsection. "We can't chance having you fall."

Likely she should have argued, but she didn't have the will. The emotion of the day had exhausted her. As he nudged the horse into a slow walk, she nestled against his chest.

His body felt rigid. Plainly, he held her only because he felt he must. She closed her eyes and listened to

the beat of his heart—a little quick, she thought. He
was a man, and she'd heard that men had automatic
responses to contact with any woman. From what she'd
heard, these responses were strong. For an instant she
was tempted to wrap her arms around him and look
up into his eyes. Somehow she sensed that if she did,
he would kiss her. But she'd gone that route before,
and, alas, both times he'd walked away from her.

She turned her thoughts back to the events of the
last two hours. It seemed like ages since she'd run
from her father's house. As they emerged from the
woods into the Park again, she said without facing
Miles, "Thank you for helping me recover the artifacts.
I . . . I'm ashamed that I ever accused you of stealing
the plate."

He snorted. "After everything you'd learned today,
you had plenty of reason for distrust."

"I had no reason to believe you a thief. I don't know
how I can ever properly apologize."

"The balance due on the apology scale is far heavier
on my side, I assure you."

She bit her lip, unable to deny how much his advising
her father to banish her had hurt her. *Why?* she wanted
to ask—but she couldn't brook hearing the answer.
Clearly, he hadn't wanted her near him. The stolen
kiss had been one of those involuntary male responses.

"There's no point in arguing about who owes whom
a greater apology," she said. "Right now we should
be concentrating on the artifacts. Let's try to enjoy this
moment, just as Papa suggested."

"You're right. That's what you deserve."

Trying to follow her own advice, she looked up at
the starlit sky and took in a deep breath of the cool
night air. The moon had risen higher, and crickets
resounded all around them. Life wasn't as bad as it
had been a few hours ago. She still had her family

and her work. The plate—and more—was back. Miles might not love her as she wished, but she had this discovery to share with him, and for tonight, it was all their own.

She closed her eyes, imagining he wanted to hold her as she did him. Something about the tension in his body felt mysterious and tempting. She sighed, pretending that he enjoyed this bumpy ride, sliding against each other, as much as she did.

Too soon, they rode up to the dig site, and he halted the horses. When he loosened his grip around her, she had no choice but to sit up straight. She made a show of straightening her skirts, then slipped down to the ground. The night felt cold without his body against hers.

While he slid off the saddle and tied both horses, she walked toward the trench. Two unlit lanterns stood at the edge, along with a tinderbox. Her father must have left them after his search of the grounds. She bent and got to work on lighting them.

"The moment of truth." Miles stepped up beside her just as she'd lit the second lantern.

Seeing that he held both canvas sacks, she picked up the lanterns and turned toward the trench. "Shall we?"

As they descended into the pit, she wished again that her project had wound up as it should have. It was bad enough that she'd thrown herself at Miles and had been rejected, but then she'd feigned an interest in Gough, too. She hated the thought of how stupid Miles must consider her. Earning regard for her intellect had always been an important aim in her life, and he was the one person from whom she most wanted it.

She set down the lanterns on either side of the trench, near the holes where the treasures had lain. Her only choice was to buckle down with her archaeological pursuits and hope eventually to regain some of his esteem that way. She refused to think about the fact that he'd never love her. For goodness' sake, she *should* have been focusing on the culmination of their project.

Miles unwrapped the plate and stooped to place it back in the hole where it had once rested. Pulling the other artifacts out of the larger sack, he stashed them in the earth as well. He brushed off his hands and looked up to her with a slight smile, his eyebrows raised as though he truly longed to please her. The expression made him appear vulnerable.

She laughed—in spite of everything. "Shall we throw some dirt on top of them, too?"

His smile widened. In the warm glow of the lamps, he looked boyish and more handsome than ever. "Unfortunately, we don't have a shovel, so we can't bury them completely."

"Be careful what you wish for. We don't want another cave-in."

"No. Don't even joke about it." He bent down and picked up the large sack, spreading it across the ground near the gaping hole. "You can use this to sit on. The ground is damp."

She glanced at the smaller bag and knew he would never fit on top of it. Sinking down on the big one, she made sure to take up only half its area. The gratifying feel of his body was fresh in her mind, and she hoped she might have just a little more of it tonight. Patting the open side, she looked up at him. "Come share with me. There's plenty of room."

His eyes widened—and not surprisingly, since the sack was less than a yard long. But just when she thought he would object, he sat down, close enough to her that she could feel the heat emanating from his body.

"Now, this is how uncovering the plate *should* have

been.'' She sighed and stretched forward to take the piece back out. Placing the artifact partly on his lap and partly on hers, she ran her fingers over the small section cleaned by Gough. "Many a housemaid would think me mad, but I cannot wait to find some polish and delve into this."

Miles bent and closely examined the item he'd been obliged to duck only an hour before. "I hope you won't decline a bit of help with the chore."

"I'm not quite so mad as *that*," she said, glad to hear that he wanted to spend more time working with her. "There's a good deal of silver here."

"Indeed there is." He gave her a warm smile.

They spent a few more minutes marveling over the plate, then examined each of the matching pieces. With each item, her awe grew. She'd never dreamed of finding a cache of artifacts this rare right in Lowery Park.

Miles' sparkling eyes showed that he shared her excitement. Giddy with success, they pointed out details in the handiwork of each piece, estimated the century of origin and speculated why the articles might have been buried outside the wall.

"This is an extraordinary find, Mellie." He set down the final article, an exquisitely crafted pitcher. "I thank you with all my heart for allowing me to help unearth it."

"Thank *me?*" She put aside a small bowl. "Miles, if not for your help with—"

"There's no need to flatter me." He cast his gaze downward with apparent self-consciousness. "I don't warrant it."

She studied his bowed head, biting her lip. What was he thinking? That he regretted ever kissing her, because he knew it had meant far more to her than to him? She wondered if he still felt any trace of attraction to her at all. Surely not enough, in any case. Why couldn't he see how perfect they'd be together? What was it about her that repelled him?

Forcing her thoughts back to their professional relationship, she said, "You worked hard, especially after the second collapse."

"After I *caused* the second collapse, you mean."

She shook her head. "I'm not going to debate with you about your worthiness now. Arguing isn't the best way to celebrate a grand discovery."

He lifted his gaze to meet hers, his expression solemn. "How *should* we celebrate it then?"

Her breath caught in her throat. The gravity of the feeling between them seemed immense—a taut line of control ready to snap. She didn't dare say a word, sure that any movement would compel him to back off, as he always did. Her only answer was an unwavering stare.

Somehow it was enough.

With his gaze fixed on her eyes, he reached out and lifted her chin. He leaned forward and met her lips with his.

She knew that she was repeating a mistake she'd made before, but she closed her eyes and melted. His mouth was hot and delicious. He deepened the kiss, and her mind whirled with pleasure and awe. Though she tried to will herself away from him, instinct took over and she matched the moves he made with hunger.

He slipped his arms around her, and she pulled him close to her, as she'd wanted to do during the ride here. Entangled in each other's limbs, they slumped to the ground, unmindful of the dirt and rubble.

The feel of his body pressed against the length of her sparked sensations of ecstasy the likes of which she had never imagined. She wanted him closer yet.

Throwing her head back, she pushed her hips upward against him.

He groaned—then suddenly pulled away. Chilly air flooded the space between them.

She opened her eyes and looked into his, her breath coming quickly.

"We must not." He pulled out of her arms and rolled over onto his back, staring up at the sky. "How many times will I take advantage of you? There can no longer be an excuse—especially after all you've been through. I don't even know what to say for myself."

Senses still reeling, she put a hand to her head and could not think how to answer.

"We'd best get back to the manor." He sat up, dragging his hands through his tousled hair.

"Wait." She grabbed his arm before he could rise. It was a beautiful evening, she was with the man she loved, and she couldn't stand to let him go so easily. But how could she possibly stop him?

He turned to her with clouded eyes that made her long to comfort him.

She searched for something to say without blurting out the entire truth. At last, she slid her fingers down his arm to rest on top of his hand. Weakly, she said, "Surely, we deserve a little more time to savor our success before sharing it with anyone else."

He sat still, watching their joined hands, yet not returning her grasp. "What we were doing a minute ago was hardly savoring success."

Staring at his profile, she needed to know—once and for all—just what their kisses meant to him. "What exactly were we doing?"

He met her gaze, his expression grim. "Frankly, Mellie, I think *you* were attempting to deny your feelings for Gough."

She felt her cheeks flush but forced herself to hold

his gaze. "And what about you? Were you trying to help me deny my feelings?"

"As if I could." He gave a humorless laugh and looked away. "I don't know what to tell you. I suppose I was just being a rogue."

She contemplated his averted face. Though she knew little about how men's minds worked, she could have sworn he was hiding something. Was there any chance he truly cared for her? She couldn't very well come out and ask him. Moistening her lips, she said instead, "I suppose you must think very little of me to treat me in such a roguish manner."

His gaze flew to meet hers, his expression startled. "You couldn't be further from the truth. That is ... you and I have worked very closely together. I assure you I hold you in the utmost respect."

"You seemed to be holding me in something else a moment ago." She paused but forced herself to trudge on. "What do you think it means when a man bestows such kisses on a woman he professes to respect?"

He took a labored breath. "I'm afraid you'll have to judge for yourself. If I thought there were any point in saying more, I would."

"Would you?" She swallowed, terrified to hope that she understood his meaning. "Well, what if I told you, at the risk of *losing* your respect, that I never had any particular feelings for Lord Gough? I, most foolishly, implied that I did, but only in a misguided attempt to ... to flaunt my femininity."

His brow furrowed. "Mellie, your sister told me how serious you were about your new suitor before I knew his identity. If you're saying this to try to hide how hurt you are—"

"Oh, Miles, I wasn't hurt by Gough, only angered. Terry just told you that because she thought it would ... it would stimulate your interest in me."

"This was a ploy cooked up by your sister?" He pressed his lips together. "It does smell of one of her antics."

"She meant well, of course. And, not knowing a whit about how to behave with men myself, I went along with it. I never suspected what a fool I was making of myself."

"No more a fool than I made of myself." He sighed. "I'm so used to dodging plots like your sister's that when a woman truly affected me, I tried to dodge that, too. That's why I urged your father to send you away early. As soon as I saw how much leaving your work upset you, I spoke to him again, but he'd made up his mind. I'm so sorry."

She gave him a half smile. "It doesn't matter now."

"No, I suppose it doesn't." He stared at her, his eyes dark and intense. "You truly never cared for Gough?"

The only times she'd ever seen that look before was directly before he kissed her. As she finally allowed herself to believe he might return her regard, her elation played at the corners of her mouth. "How much could I feel for a man with no natural interest in archaeology?"

He stared at her a moment longer, then broke into a grin. "I can hardly believe what I'm hearing. Mellie, let's make sure we have no further misunderstandings. You once told me you have no intention of marrying— but I do share your devotion to archaeology, and I'd be happy to stay on working at the villa as long as you wish. I also love you to distraction. Given all these factors, might you possibly consider marrying me?"

She beamed at him. "I've been considering little else for a month now."

"Does that mean you will?"

"Yes. I'd love to."

He took her in his arms, and they fell back on the ground, sealing their declaration with a kiss.

After a few moments, she lay her head on his chest, quietly enjoying their personal triumph. "Is this not wonderful? A confirmed bachelor and a hopeless hoyden, suddenly brought together for good."

"Mmm," he murmured.

"And if that weren't enough to set all our acquaintances on their ears, we have an incredible discovery to announce as well. It turned out just as you wished in the toast you made the night before I left the Park. I'll wager that we truly *have* made the greatest find of the year."

"Of a lifetime, I should say." He pulled her closer and kissed the tip of her nose.

"Do you really think so? That in the next half a century no one will unearth a greater treasure than our little silver collection?"

"I *know* no one will unearth a greater treasure than *I* have, but I'm not speaking of those trifles." He waved a dismissing hand toward the artifacts. "*My* treasure is one who *chooses* to bury herself in this villa. I'm only thankful I was a skilled enough archaeologist to find her."

A NOTE FROM THE AUTHOR

Giovanni Batista Belzoni explored Egypt in the early nineteenth century and uncovered some of the most important of the ancient tombs, including that of Seti I. He really did stage an exhibition in Regency London, but the account of the event in *Lord St. Leger's Find* is entirely fictional. Belzoni, however, was a former circus strong man and certainly would have had a sense of how to put on a good show. He was also known for scrawling his name in large letters on the tombs he found.

Having finished up *Lord St. Leger's Find,* I'm now working on my next Regency romance for Zebra. For current news on my books, please visit my website at *www.geocities.com/jennifermalin.*

Thank you for reading!

Jennifer Malin